dixi
books

## Micheál Lovett

Micheál Lovett is an Irish writer and teacher, who has written acclaimed work in theatre, radio and TV, both in Ireland and internationally. His work has been nominated for the Stewart Parker Award.

He has called Ireland, Spain, US, UK and Australia home over the last twenty years. As a playwright his work has been produced in Ireland, London and the United States. A founding member of Blood in the Alley theatre company, he explores the magic realism between the physical and the spiritual.

Micheál was raised in the seanachaí tradition of Irish storytelling and possesses a deep love of nature and its connections with spirituality and mythology. He brings this knowledge and dramatic experience to bear in his debut novel Realm of the Hare.

He lives with his wife and daughter between Australia and Ireland.

# Realm of the Hare

Micheál Lovett

**Dixi Books**

Realm of the Hare
Writer: Micheál Lovett
Editor: Gina Edwards
Proofreading: Gina Edwards
Cover Design: Natalia Klimchuk
Design: Pablo Ulyanov
1st Edition: April 2021

ISBN: 978-1-913680-14-5
1. Young Adult Fiction 2. Fantasy 3. Magical Realism
4. Fight for Nature

© Dixi Books Publishing
293 Green Lanes, Palmers Green, London, England, N13 4XS
info@dixibooks.com
www.dixibooks.com

# Realm of the Hare

## Micheál Lovett

dixi books

*The Voice of the New Age*

To John and Sue, Sarah and Bou, and my family.


With special thanks to Kevin O'Connor

*"Come forth into the light of things,*
*Let Nature be your teacher."*
William Wordsworth

# Prologue

The scratching of pen on paper gave sound to the feverish turnings of her mind. Dr Sarah Moriarty looked up and saw the peaceful snow fall through the darkness, flakes coming to rest on the sill of her mullioned window. She sensed a presence out there. Something that was a stranger to the world.

The boiling kettle clicked and she turned her head from a table ladened with open books. She instinctually looked to the cot beside her and the sleeping, six-week-old baby that lay snug under a blanket. Sarah bent forward and kissed the brow of the child and breathed in the newness that came from the baby's cradle.

Pouring boiled water into the mug, the teabag coloured the water as she dunked it slowly. She stood in the studio kitchen of her apartment in Oxford, just a stone's throw away from the Celtic studies department. It was big enough for Sarah, her studies and her newborn. There was little room for extravagance, but it was warm and homely.

Taking the teabag from the cup she turned and froze. In front of her was the massive form of a black Grizzly bear standing as tall as the ceiling and as wide as the doorway. The monstrous animal was blocking the way to her child. Sarah's only thought was that of her baby, who lay in the room next door. On the Grizzly's head were the massive horns of a ram. The kitchen light bounced off the sheen of the animal's mane.

'Hello, Sarah' the animal said, in a deep sonorous voice.

Briefly rocked onto her heels, Sarah spilt some tea as she leaned against the sink. Behind her, she located a carving knife and held it tightly in her hand, unseen to the animal. It stared in silence, yellow eyes in which swirled the colours of moving lava, its canines proud from beneath lips on the side of its mouth, curved out like tusks. Sarah kept the tea in her hand and didn't move a muscle.

'Pejanen Tyger,' said Sarah, with a smile, holding the knife tighter still. 'It's been twenty years.'

The giant beast gave a deep growl.

'Many lifetimes for me,' he replied, as he scratched his massive chest.

'Are you alone?' Sarah asked.

'Yes. We need to talk.'

'If you'll excuse me.' Sarah nodded and moved past the animal to her baby, the knife shielded by her hip.

The animal climbed down onto all fours. Its gnarled claws tapped on the parquet floor as they landed.

'Would you like a cup of tea? It's juniper,' said Sarah, over her shoulder, still holding the knife.

'Yes. A cup would be too small, would you have a bucket?' said Pejanen Tyger, as he tried to turn in the kitchen, knocking his horns against cupboard doors and fridge magnets.

Sarah sipped her tea and looked on as the giant bear lapped up the juniper tea from the biggest saucepan she had. His tongue was vigourous and his teeth clinked against the side of the saucepan. She held her child tightly in her arms.

'Nice place,' said the horned bear.

'Perfect for us.'

He licked his saucepan clean, leaned back and stopped suddenly when he heard the crack of the chair frame. It was clear that this ancient animal was far too big for the room and its furniture.

'Sorry about that,' said Pejanen, embarrassed by his clumsiness.

'It's ok,' replied Sarah, 'it was old anyway.'

'Do you know why I'm here?' said the bear.

Sarah nodded as she softly rocked the baby.

'You knew this day would come,' he added.

Sarah nodded again, not taking her eyes off the animal.

He opened his massive claw and presented a blue vial. Even in the half light it glowed, filled with a liquid. Placing it on the coffee table, he glanced to her with deep intent in his eyes. She looked to the vial.

'The Skiah?' Sarah said, inquisitively.

'Yes.'

'Why do I need the shield?'

'To protect you.'

'From what?

'From who? Is the question you should be asking Sarah.'

Pejanen Tyger repositioned his ample rump on the floor. 'Mustela grows stronger with every moment. He chases the secrets you have, searches for you and will probably find you. It's time to pass them on.'

The bear didn't finish his sentence and just looked at the child in Sarah's arms. He peered in closer and saw one of the baby's feet appearing from underneath the swaddling blanket. It was an unusual shape. Sarah saw this and looked directly at him. The bear raised his head and nodded.

'What is her name?'

'Boudicca.'

'Strong,' the grizzly growled. 'You must take the Skiah and sleep next to her and as you sleep, the secrets will pass between you.'

'I don't want to bring her into this.'

'You have no choice. You are Ullanite. I wish it to be different, but the future of all depends on it.'

There was an uncomfortable silence between them. The bear got back on all fours and took a step toward Sarah; he lowered his head presenting his forehead in reverence. Sarah lowered her head too, leaned forward and placed her forehead against his. The moment hung there and the baby looked up, raising her hand and touched the tusk of the mighty beast.

'Somnia Sine Metu,' the animal said, in a low voice. It took a little time for him to leave, as the door was too tight. His hips bumped on the framework, shaking pictures on the walls, his rump moving the baby's buggy a few inches. Once out though, the door shut quickly behind him.

From behind her back Sarah took out the knife and placed it on the edge of the coffee table. She picked up the vial and then whispered to the child.

'Somnia Sine Metu.'

◆　　✦　　◆

13

'You've reached the voicemail of Dr. Sarah Moriarty, Professor of Celtic studies, Oxford University. I'm afraid I can't get to your call right now, but please leave a message and I will get back to you as soon as possible.'

BEEP

'Mum, pizza or pasta, let me know, byyyyye.'

BEEP

'Mum, where are you? I've put on a pizza, don't be surprised if it's finished when you get home.'

BEEP

'Mum, where are you? I'm getting worried. I've finished the pizza. Told ya!'

BEEP

'Mum, I've called the police. I'm getting really worried. Please call me immediately.'

BEEP

'Sarah this is your father. Just got a call from Boudicca, she's worried about you. Call her as soon as you can, or call me too. You know the number.'

BEEP

'Dr. Sarah Moriarty. This is Police Constable Akton. We are looking to locate your whereabouts. Your daughter and parents have expressed their worry. Contact us as soon as you can.'

BEEP

'Mum. Mum! Please pick up.'

# Chapter 1

The Book of Megrez

*Chapter 27*
*Verse 612*

*On the child of bears*

*At the rising of the ninth moon, on the coldest and shortest days,
I wake and quiver and feel the pain crash over me. I heave, breathe
and wait. If the way is not impeded, when the moon falls there will
be two cubs born from me. If the great Bradán deems it so, then I
will give birth to a child, all will be blind and toothless and will
suckle, before destiny calls The Ursine to its fate.*

It is in quiet moments fear roars.

Boudicca sat clipped into her seat, her mousy brown hair a
mass of unruly curls, exploding out and down to her shoulders.
Her skin was the colour of ivory keys, her face sprinkled with
freckles. The plane shuddered above the roar of engines as the
wheels touched down. Smiles of relief bloomed on passenger's
faces, accompanied by the growing cacophony of beeping phones.

Boudicca took a moment to herself and breathed deeply as
flying made her anxious. She drew her hands across her face
and then looked out the window, spying Cork airport. Teeming
ground staff in their low-riding vehicles and high visibility vests
scurried around the plane's giant wheels.

The thought of ants at work crossed her mind for the briefest
of moments. These days very little remained in her head because
Boudicca Moriarty was tired, sleep was a stranger. She was twelve
years old, with a mother who had disappeared without a trace,
three days earlier.

She followed the clicking heels of the flight attendant, who led her from the plane to the terminal. In her jacket and skirt uniform, the attendant presented herself bejeweled and lipsticked with a high beam smile surrounded by fake tan that was rich on the cheek but thin on the neck. She talked in a chain of statements and questions, never once expecting to be answered or challenged.

'Did you have fun?' the attendant enquired, rabbiting on without waiting for Boudicca's reply. 'Planes are exciting. Are you on your own? Is it your first flight? Do you live in London?' The flight attendant barely drew breath. 'I love London. I'm a terror for the shopping! And of course, the shows, I love the shows!'

Boudicca looked at the attendant's teeth, and the traces of lipstick that smudged there with her prattle. She handed Boudicca over to a waiting ground staff lady. The ground staff were a different breed in the airport world, rooted and earthbound. This groundling lady had a guinea pig frown that was as constant as November-rain. Her make-up was crudely applied, plain short hair trimmed and neat, comfy in her safe shoes and no-nonsense nails. She, unlike the flight attendant, was gravity's slave.

The flight attendant offered the groundling paper work, looking above her with a confidence that seemed divine. This creature of the air seemed to avoid any physical contact with grounding. She smiled exuberantly and walked away in her high heels, magisterially ignoring all the attention she drew in on herself. Her chin up, as if in a constant yearning to return to the sky, where she believed she belonged.

The groundling was a simple woman. Her head was naturally cranked to the sound of her walkie-talkie as she led Boudicca, with short slow steps, through the brightly lit airport. She looked back to Boudicca with widened eyes as she saw the child walk behind her. She was still frowning.

Even with her corrective heel, Boudicca's limp made her stand out. The soles of her shoes slipped a little on the polished floor. Boudicca had long given up the thought of girls being light on their feet; her dreams of being a ballerina hadn't even the courage to enter her head anymore.

She was lame and shod like a dray horse, bent and uneven. Boudicca was used to the looks by now and never commented or even tried to mask it. One leg was shorter than the other by about an inch. Numerous operations as a toddler and child failed to correct the discrepancy, and so she was resigned to wearing a shoe with a bigger heel that accommodated her imperfection as a badge of difference. The groundling desired to help Boudicca, or at least to be seen to help her.

'Let me do that for you, there love,' the lady announced, her November-rain frown faltering as she grabbed the handle of the suitcase.

Boudicca didn't let the handle go and protested she was fine and could do it on her own.

The groundling insisted. 'It's my job sure. You might as well.' She went to grab the suitcase again.

This time sharply and with as much manners as she could muster, Boudicca pulled the suitcase away. 'Thank you for your help, but I insist,' she sternly replied. Her English accent added a barbed tone to Boudicca's voice.

The November-rain frown on the groundling's face melted, replaced by a resting dour expression, surprised by the child's perceived ungratefulness.

'Suit yourself,' she said, looking at Boudicca limp away.

The doors leading to the arrivals hall slid open with a whoosh and a group of people stood in front of Boudicca, greeting and hugging the new arrivals. Trills of happiness and excitement accompanied announcements of boarding gates on the loudspeaker above their heads. Hesitant manly handshakes gathered beside free embraces and tears.

Boudicca scanned the gathering of people, looking for a recognisable face. She smiled as she saw Prospero Moriarty, her grandfather, amongst the crowd. He stood calmly, a thin man in his seventies. Bright blue eyes sparkled out from a wrinkled face, white windy hair untended and wild. The buttons on his shirt were fastened off-kilter, his tie askew. Like his granddaughter, this old man, too, was a little off balance.

Upon seeing her, Prospero went down on one knee with his arms opened wide. Boudicca dropped her suitcase and ran to him in a lame stride. One of the straps on her backpack slipped off her shoulder, it hung jingling and lopsided. Others looked on, privately warmed by the depth of emotion between the old man and the young girl as they hugged, softening into each other's embrace. They held themselves there for a while, neither spoke, only sniffles from the muffled ball of a hug.

Boudicca felt her grandfather's stubble on her cheek and she buried her nose in the consoling touch of his shoulder and frayed collar. The intoxicant smell of spices, liniments and ointments coming from his jacket brought back happy memories. These were the odours of his profession, the healing of animals and the setting of bones. There was convalescence in the smell.

Her own joints relaxed of their tightness, the ball and socket of her hips and shoulders seemed to sit more snugly than before. This was her first embrace of love in days and Boudicca did her best to stay there as long as she could, taking nothing for granted anymore.

Prospero pulled himself back and held her at arms length, looking at her face and smiling. 'Boudicca my child! How you have grown. I'm sorry we meet under these circumstances.' His eyes were calm yet focused, scanning her brow, wiping away her small tears with his farming thumbs.

'Yeah,' Boudicca said, wiping her nose with her sleeve, unsure of where to look. Then it occurred to her that she had not turned on her phone since arriving. She quickly stripped off her backpack and unzipped it, took out a phone and turned it on. 'See if mum's texted me,' said Boudicca, without raising her head, waiting for the screen to power up.

Prospero waited for his granddaughter to finish.

There was a ping that came through and Boudicca's eyes lit with delight. 'It's a message!'

Prospero became animated as well, ignorant of new technology. 'What does it say?'

Boudicca held the phone, her hands trembling, and then closed it immediately without saying a word.

'What is it?' asked Prospero.

'It's a welcome message from a phone company,' said Boudicca, her voice wounded by hope.

'Don't worry,' said Prospero, 'your mother will contact you, when she can.'

Even though in his senior years, Prospero was strong limbed

and a striking character, his figure and features were like granite hewn by the weather, a lifetime of sheep farming on mountainsides, smoothing his hard edges.

After a moment, the groundling arrived, pulling Boudicca's suitcase behind her, with a sheet of paper in her hand. 'In the commotion, you dropped your case,' she said, self-satisfied at the assistance provided, casting her eyes to a nearby group, witnesses to her professional kindness.

'Thank you,' said Boudicca.

'Delighted to help a brave little trooper like yourself, finally,' said the groundling, with a lingering look.

'Prospero Moriarty?' the lady asked. 'Have you got any identification?'

'I do,' he said.

There was a pause. 'Could you show me it please?' she asked.

Prospero smiled, presented his driver's licence and signed the sheet allowing the lady to relinquish the child and her responsibilities.

'Prospero? Unusual name.'

'Is it? What's your name?'

'Mary,' replied the groundling.

'Makes two of us.'

A loud indecipherable call came through on her walkie-talkie, and Prospero took advantage of the break, calmly stealing the suitcase from the groundling and walking away with his grandchild. Boudicca held Prospero's hand as tightly as she could, feeling the hard skin of his palms.

Outside the terminal, they walked past people smoking in designated areas, hemmed in like cattle waiting calmly for the bullet. Arriving at the car, Prospero put her suitcase in the boot and opened the back door, inviting Boudicca to climb in. The smell from the car was an even more intense mixture of Prospero's medicinal creations.

To her surprise, and no little delight, sitting in the back seat was a fully-grown hare. She thought it a rabbit at first, but it stood more upright and its outline was clearly different to that of a rabbit, more distinguished and leonine. The hare looked at Boudicca with dark interrupted eyes as if contemplating something of great importance, convincing her of its wildness. He thumped his paw twice on the pan of the seat and then looked away.

'Meet Finn,' said Prospero, banging the driver's door a few times, the distended seat belt catching in the latch. 'Don't pet him, until he gets used to you. He's wild and wild hares are fearless.'

'Wild?' said Boudicca.

'He could rob a bank, that fella,' said Prospero, as he shut the door and turned the key, laying the seat belt across his body without latching it to the clasp. 'Fearless.' Prospero looked cautiously in the rear-view mirror.

'I didn't know you kept animals, Granddad.'

'Finn is keeping me, more like,' said Prospero.

'Finn.' Boudicca looked at the hare and considered the name.

For the first part of the journey, she couldn't help but stare at Finn, who stood on his back legs, paws on the door trying to get a better look at the passing countryside. His ears flopped over the back of his head, giving him a look of sleek intelligence and self-possession. When the wonder had worn off, Boudicca joined him, looking out her own window, she soon became numbed by the blurring ditches and slow-rolling fields in the mid-distance.

Arriving at the farm, Boudicca's Grandmother, Nonie Moriarty was wringing her hands. She heard the car coming up the road from the open door of the cottage and ran out to welcome the arrivals. Short and grey-haired, having just reached her seventies, Nonie was spritely in frame and blessed with the energy of a person half her age. With high cheeks and a cherry-shaped nose, there was an obvious lineage between Boudicca and her Grandmother.

Boudicca was barely out of the car before she was smothered in a hug. No words were spoken, silence and sniffing were all that accompanied the warm embrace, as her grandmother drew her hand across Boudicca's face and then kissed each cheek affectionately. Taking her by the hand, Boudicca was led to the old cottage, and while as of yet unable to speak, Nonie pointed out all the flowers that bloomed in the garden, the boundaries of which were edged with stone from old outhouses that once dotted the yard. Boudicca held onto Nonie as tight as she could, gaining strength from the touch.

The Moriarty's cottage was surrounded by a farmyard and

outhouses that lay on the banks of Lough Leane, with Nonie's garden backing onto Killarney National Park, Tomies wood and O'Sullivan's Cascade close by. The house edged an expanse of nature reserve filled with forests and gorse, a haven for animals and ancient trees. The park was a natural arcadia, and as Boudicca walked past the lake, the view of the mountains beyond, she sighed. The very sight calming her, the buzz of meadow bees and chirping swallows were a liniment to her fretful soul.

Warm tea and slices of that morning's soda bread with boiled eggs and ham were placed before Boudicca, which she gobbled down with a lusty hunger. From the corner of the kitchen, Maurice Fitzgerald, her grandparent's black and white cat, sat languidly on the soft chair warmed by the small slow combustion fire, taking the cold edge out of the working kitchen. The white wall behind the fire was blackened from the heat and dust of the firebox and exposed flue, above it sat a mighty oak lintel that showed its cracks, grain and edge in silent pride.

On the other side of the fire sat Finn, the hare pointedly looking down at the cat. Maurice Fitzgerald ignored the imperious stand of this princely hare with indifference and deigned to sleep in front of him. The hare did not appreciate the lack of respect, but Maurice Fitzgerald was Maurice Fitzgerald, and like all cats, was tamed only by his own wildness. Boudicca marvelled at Finn's presence in such a domestic setting.

'I'll say no more, Boudicca,' said Nonie, interrupting Boudicca's thoughts, 'only that it's a mystery what has happened to your mother. And I'll say no more. I've made your bed in the top room and you can put your things there when you're ready and I'll say no more.' Nonie sped up her delivery of the last sentence, the words tapering off, her throat tightening as she retired to the privacy of the pantry, wishing none to see her cry.

Boudicca could hear her, yet felt no desire to invade that privacy, and sat eating the last of her egg.

'We've been in contact with the Police in England,' said Prospero, 'they've assured us that they will contact us if anything changes.'

Boudicca nodded.

'It's not Oxford, but you can call this place home for as long as you wish,' he added, as he looked to the window. Boudicca thought the light coming through seemed to gather up the pieces of this old man. Pieces that would disassemble at a moment's notice, if he let himself think too much.

Boudicca smiled at the reassurance he tried to offer, but worried at the gravity of the circumstances. She saw her grandparent's age more than ever before. 'Granddad, I am sad but happy to be here. Do you understand what I'm saying?'

Without looking at her, Prospero nodded in the sunlight, his eyes glistening, tears sitting on his lashes, his gaze unmoving as if trying to see through the sun.

•     ✦     •

The bedroom felt strange as Boudicca sat on the queen-size mattress, the brass frame was smooth to the touch. There was coldness in the room from having recently been aired for the new arrival. In the corner, freshly cut flowers fought valiantly to banish shadows; primrose, moon daisies, geraniums and scarlet pimpernels seemed to be crowded on all sides by the darkness of the old house. There was a little desk beside the bed, a reading lamp on it.

Boudicca unzipped her suitcase and started to stow away her clothes. Taking out her black leather boots, she looked at them. Like all her shoes, one was normal, the other was shod with a thicker heel to accommodate her deformity. She disliked their lack of sameness, more like sister and older brother than identical twins. Even though they helped her walk, she thought them ugly. This was the constant drone of her life, she needed a break from it at times, and walking in her bare feet or regular shoes helped. She placed the shoes neatly against the wall and studiously ignored them.

She maneuvered the now empty suitcase into a space at the bottom of the wardrobe. It seemed to fit, but annoyingly the door wouldn't close. She moved the case in the space numerous ways, and leaning in her shoulder, pushed the door against it, finding the latch just out of reach. She tried another helpful push, but once again, the door refused to close. Worryingly, she heard a crack.

Unsure of what she had done to the furniture that was old and of great sentimental value, she surveyed the damage. Removing the case, she saw a panel askew. As she tried to put it back into place, it fell away completely in her hand, revealing a cavity behind. Inside the dark recess an unlikely item glistened.

It was a square silver locket, the size of her thumb, attached to a chain. Taking it out she saw its fine edges and smooth finish. On the front and back there were little markings like dots. With her small fingers, Boudicca easily opened the clasp.

Inside sat a perfectly snug, yet tiny wine coloured leather-bound notebook. Boudicca saw an embossed golden star on the cover. She opened the metal lock that clicked with the pressing of a brass stud, revealing the pages within. She was amazed to see tiny writing that was illegible. Removing the book, she found beneath it a shard of paper on which there was writing. She recognised it immediately as her mother's hand.

> *'Let no one see this ancient star,*
> *Desired by many near and far.*
> *Times will come both foul and fair,*
> *The secret lies with this wild hare.'*

Boudicca took a moment to consider the message. It meant nothing to her. At the desk beside the bed she flicked on the lamp and looked at the book again. Excitedly, she went to her pencil case and took out a magnifying glass. Finding the perfect magnification, she gazed on the first page. There she saw two words in a bold script that were recognisable. "ULLAUNS". And beneath that, the word "MEGREZ".

On the other pages, made big by the magnifying glass, every available space was covered in script, the words unfamiliar to Boudicca – not English, not Irish, not Latin. But the handwriting was her mother's, that she did know. Boudicca was used to this. Her mother was a trained linguist, and so it wasn't unusual to see shards of paper around their Oxford apartment, scrawled in different and ancient languages. Already learning Gaelic and Latin in her spare time, Boudicca was open to new words and enjoyed their sounds.

However, this book was unlike anything she had seen and was now the last connection she had to her mother. Something Boudicca could return to and appraise, even if it was impossible to understand. It was her mother and it was alive, not yet a memory and she wished it to remain so, and by this extension her mother was alive.

*'Times will come both foul and fair,*
*The secret lies with this wild hare*

Boudicca heard the bedroom door creak open. She quickly closed the book and replaced it in the locket, clasping it tight in her hand. Looking at the door, it took time for the figure to appear. She heard the light patter of soft feet on the floorboards. It was Finn, bending his head around the doorframe.

'Oh it's you. Bored with Maurice Fitzgerald, are you?' said Boudicca, moving onto the bed.

The hare entered and in one bound landed on the bed. Standing there, he looked at her with a deep interest that surprised Boudicca.

'You're looking at me deeply Finn.'

He continued to stare.

'It's not mannerly to stare,' she pressed.

With that, Finn seemed to recognise his impudence and turned his body a little. She smiled and wondered whether he could understand her. 'Can you understand me?'

He ignored her, sniffing the bedclothes, his nose twitching.

She patted the bedspread, encouraging him to come closer.

Finn did nothing.

'Shake my hand.' Boudicca offered her hand, but Finn ignored it. She thought better of pursuing this and placed her uneven legs on the bedcover. Finn moved to accommodate her limbs. 'Thank you,' she said.

The hare investigated both her feet with loud sniffs that were heard above the silence of the room. She looked down to see him consider the difference in both her feet.

'They're uneven,' she said. 'Just so you know.'

Finn paused and began to sniff the smaller leg, which seemed to be of greater interest to him. He rose onto his back legs and moved his front paws, as if dancing or boxing shadows.

'What are you doing?' She pulled her legs away, more aware now of his wildness.

He stopped and calmly made his way up the quilt cover with ponderous hops. She moved her hand to afford him space and he scaled her hip to lie on her tummy. She felt the sharpness of his claws as he walked softly across her, where he curled up and immediately closed his eyes, falling comfortably asleep. She sank her fingers gently into his fur feeling his warm belly rise with each breath. A snore soon emanated from the ball of fluff. Not long after, Boudicca became drowsy. She closed her weary eyes as her fingers tightened around the locket.

# Chapter 2

The Book of Mizar

*Chapter 8004*
*Verse 9*

*Young swallows feasting*

*Between the fourth and fifth moon, I see them rising on the warmth above flowering meadows. My young are quiet for the moment, their throats full as I leave the perch of my mud-packed nest. I swoop down and turn and turn again and sweep and they're ignorant of their fate, as I gather them on the wing. Midges, flies, gads, butterfly. I leave the meadow and reel along hedgerow, toward a copse; seek out life, which can be sacrificed. I return to the perch and let my young tear at my beak with their hungry trills, some taking legs others taking wings, I pack their throats again, and they are quiet for a moment, their throats full again as I leave the perch of my mud-packed nest.*

'He's gone. Where's he gone? The wild hare has gone. Finn has gone!'

Boudicca woke to the sound of Prospero calling her from the kitchen.

She looked down and saw the vacancy on her belly where Finn had been, the area still warm. Unsure of how long she had slept, Boudicca checked her watch and saw it as only five minutes. She felt the locket nestled in her hand. She put it back in the wardrobe's secret compartment and left the room feeling brighter in mind and better for the rest.

'Will you join me in my office?' Prospero called up the hallway.

Boudicca knew the office was his shed, where he treated the animals of local farmers. He took a familial pride in his trade as he was descended from a long line of bonesetters and healers. Prospero had an encyclopedic knowledge of wild flowers, plants and mushrooms and understood their medicinal qualities for both animal and man alike.

Many claimed that both Nonie and Prospero Moriarty had gifts. Some farmers would come to Prospero before going to the vet. He never thought himself in competition with science, more in compliment with other services. However, he found plenty of success where science had failed, and those who believed in his gifts were rarely disappointed and often rewarded.

Boudicca followed him across the yard. Between them, Maurice Fitzgerald dabbed his feline feet on the patches of gravel. When the shed door opened, Boudicca was assailed by the smells of natural herbs hanging from the walls, dried and readied for Prospero's oils and unctions. Inside was lit by a row of bulbs, tacked to the rafters by electrical wire and the electrical fittings dressed in bridal veils of cobwebs. An unlit still sat in the corner waiting to extract essences and ingredients from plants, to be mixed with Prospero's ancient knowledge. On one of the shelves Boudicca spied a beaten-up tin of pipe tobacco still there from the last time she visited. Along the side of the small tin, it read "Mick Mc Quaid Cut Plug". When all else was in flux, she liked noticing these little constants.

Along the walls were jars and bottles of every sort, standing sentry and jostling for space. The substances within them could bring an end to colic, the shakes, fevers and infections. There were remedies and concoctions that coaxed animals back to health. This was a magical place to Boudicca. Her earliest memories were of sitting on a high stool near the bench, helping Prospero with his potions.

After some time, Finn arrived at the door and climbed the chair with the utmost confidence and from there to the bench. He sat himself within arm's reach of Boudicca. Maurice gave him a scant look, thinking him usurper and unwanted.

'There you are Finn,' she said, 'I was wondering where you'd got to.'

'Seems like you have a friend there,' Prospero said.

'Are you sure he's wild, Granddad?' She curiously stroked

him, seeing his eyes close as he enjoyed the rub.

'Wild as the wind child,' Prospero said.

'He arrived one day and has been here ever since. Never stopped him, but he's chosen to stay, for now anyway. I've never seen him attach himself to anybody before though. Not like you. He seems tame beside you.'

Boudicca was happy to hear this, another surprise that she had not banked on.

'Is he from the park?'

'Oh yeah. Tis full of them sure.' Prospero put some herbs into a pestle and began to grind them down with a wrist twist. 'Oh the wild hare is a sacred animal for sure,' Prospero said, his voice inflected by the endeavour of his work. 'In olden times they were admired for their beauty and cleverness, so much so that it was illegal to eat them. Sure Julius Caesar wrote that down, so it must be true.'

Boudicca looked at Finn and wondered what Julius Caesar would have thought of him.

'There are stories as to their magical powers too,' Prospero added. 'Shape shifters, small warriors, the bringers of bad news.'

Boudicca thought a moment. 'You mean there could be more bad news to come?'

Prospero stopped grinding; the mood had changed, the reality of the situation invading their little corner of work and stories. He felt silly for his lack of consideration. 'I'm sorry Boudicca. I didn't mean ….' He fumbled over words, 'I mean … they're just stories.'

Boudicca looked at the hare and continued to stroke its warm fur. 'What are you working on?'

'An unction for Paddy Kennedy from over the mountains in Camp, his chestnut mare has a fever. Tried all the antibiotics known to science and beyond and she's still getting worse.'

'What are you using?' Boudicca asked.

'Oh, simple things now like cloves, a penn'rth of sage, ten blades of grass from a field with three sides, vetch, eye bright, honeysuckle. Six drops of St John's. Two hairs from a dog that's been chased by a cat, and two hairs from a cat that's been chased by a mouse.' Prospero delivered the last line with a wink as he walked outside the shed, singing quietly to himself and catching something unseen. 'And one fist full of this!' he said, returning with a clenched fist.

'What is that?'

'The Wind,' said Prospero, opening his hand and slowly emptying the invisible contents into the pestle.

'Just wind?'

'No ordinary wind of course, sure that would be madness,' he assured her. 'A special wind. A north wind that blows from the south, if you get my meaning.' He looked at her and smiled, the pestle began to grind again.

'Grandad …'

'Yes, child?'

'What is the Ullauns?'

Prospero stopped and went to an old recipe from a frayed handwritten book, giving him time to hide the effect of the question. 'The Ullauns? The forest in the park you mean? Sure you know that. Near the Old Kenmare Road, south of Galway's River.'

'I know. But does it mean anything else?' Boudicca pressed further.

Prospero tried to look busy and unperturbed, and put more weight on the mortar. 'Peculiar question, why do you ask?'

However much he tried to hide it, Boudicca could sense he was unsettled. She felt Finn stiffen beneath her hand, his eyes opening, turning his head to the Bonesetter. 'Mum was talking a lot about it before she went missing.'

He stopped grinding and looked to the shelving in front of him. 'It depends. The Ullauns is not a *thing* per se. It is a place. Not far from here. It is an ancient forest in the park, dating from the age of ice and even before it. Filled with oaks, many oaks and alders, and …'

'And?'

'Magic. Powerful. That's what the old people used to say round here,' whispered Prospero. 'Light and dark, good and evil. You'd never find a priest or a doctor in there, let me tell you. No place for God or impericals in that wood.'

Boudicca looked to Finn.

'What did your Mum say about it?

'Oh, I can't remember. She'd tell me stories about it, when she was young. How happy she was.'

Prospero nodded his head, taking the pestle in hand. 'She was drawn to it, your mother. The Ullauns, I mean' he said, getting lost in memory. 'She'd head out in the morning and not return for hours, but she was never lost, you always knew where she was. A place of great beauty and power is the Ullauns. Has to be treated with care though. Places like that have a mind of their own, you know?'

Boudicca nodded.

'Is that all?' asked Prospero.

'One more thing. What is Megrez?'

Prospero pulled his head back, raising a jowl of surprise beneath his chin. 'The only Megrez I know, is the star. Part of the Plough.'

'The Plough?'

'Yeah, some call it the Big Bear. Ursa Major in the night sky.'

They were interrupted by the sound of a car pulling into the yard.

'That'll be Paddy,' Prospero said, hearing the crunch of Paddy's canary yellow Ford Cortina on the gravel, his blue horsebox attached.

'Prospero,' called Paddy, from the opened door of his car, one leg sticking out, and his old body rising from the seat in installments.

'Paddy,' replied Prospero, meeting him in the yard with a shake of the hand, 'how's the mare?'

Paddy took a moment and looked to the gravel. 'Poorly now, poorly.' Worry etched on Paddy's face as he looked to the horsebox, his hair combed back with Brylcreem, greasy tufts of stubble on the boundary of his cheeks and earlobes. 'She's been shaking, paying no heed to medicine.'

'Leave her here with me Paddy,' Prospero said, 'I'll do me best.'

'Sure, I know you will,' came Paddy Kennedy's resigned voice. Going to the horsebox and standing on the rusted mudguard, both men looked in on the shivering horse.

'Back her up there, like a good man,' Prospero said, as he jumped off the mudguard.

Boudicca looked on.

'Oh, Paddy, this is Boudicca.'

'Is that Sarah's young one in England? You're the spit of your mother child and your grandmother at the same age,' Paddy said.

Boudicca smiled at the recognition.

'Have you the gift like your grandfather?'

'Don't know.'

'She's an apprentice, Paddy,' Prospero said.

'Make sure he pays you. Write a contract. Get it in ink girl!' Smiling with a wink to Prospero, then Paddy redressed his face with instant gloom and walked to the car.

•      ✦      •

Later that day, the sunset was measured and long in its decline, as if time poured slowly in the bruising light. Boudicca rubbed the flour in her hands and lightly dusted her fingers before continuing to knead sourdough bread with Nonie in the kitchen. Boudicca felt the warm alms of baking smells and a calmness leaven inside her like the loaves in the oven. She noticed the ticking clock on the wall for the first time.

'Is that fella ever going to let you out of his sight?' Nonie said, her hands and chin covered in flour, looking at Finn on the chair.

'I doubt it,' Boudicca smiled.

Before heading for bed, Boudicca turned and took time to look at Nonie again, washing the mixing bowls in silence, wanting to freeze the moment, so it could be thawed out at a later date. Nonie, unaware she was being watched, sluiced out the inside of the bowl first and then dried it in a routine that was as familiar and reassuring as Boudicca remembered. The smell of the cooling bread on racks wafted through the house. Boudicca slipped away to her room, collecting the locket from the wardrobe.

With magnifying glass in hand, she began to carefully leaf through the tiny pages of the book. The writing was unmistakably her mother's and Boudicca felt drawn even though she could not understand it. As she grew tired, she held the locket in her hand. The door creaked again and in walked Finn, jumping with one bound onto the bedspread. She was more comfortable in his company now. Both dozed to the far-off sounds of Nonie listening to reels and jigs on Kerry radio.

Sometime later, Boudicca was woken abruptly to a tapping sound on her bedroom window. Raising her head from her pillow, she saw Finn perched on the windowsill, lit by a strong moon outside. She waited a moment and then saw him rise to his back legs, tapping the windowpane with his front paws, an echo of the sound that woke her. Sensing he wished to return to the wild, Boudicca wrapped herself in her nightgown and made her way to the window giving him a soft pat on his head. 'I understand Finn. You must return.'

Unhooking the latch and pushing open the window, Boudicca felt the cold night air flow into the room. Finn didn't move. He just looked at her for a moment and then slowly turned to peer out. She followed his gaze. There, to her amazement, was a most arresting sight. A fully-grown male deer stood on the dew-covered grass, snorting lightly and motionless in his immensity. Easily the height of two men, his antlers extended him to an even greater height. Wide-eyed, Boudicca noticed a white stripe on his forehead. He was close enough for her to see the blackness of his eyes, and even in the moonlight she could make out the brown mane on his shoulders and neck.

She looked to Finn, who was staring at the animal silently, and in the distance she heard the shriek of an owl from the woods. Boudicca was unsure whether she was dreaming or not. Finn leapt out the window, clearing heavy-headed flowers and hopped with purpose toward the deer, moving to his legs and barely reaching halfway up the beast's shin. The deer lowered his head, placing his muzzle in front of the hare.

To Boudicca's amazement, Finn made his way up to the deer's head, scaling its forehead, and inched along the ridge of his neck, finally coming to rest snuggly in the hollow between the deer's shoulders. It was a calm and familiar routine to the small animal.

In the way of the young, Boudicca wrestled with the idea to get her phone and take a picture, as no one would believe what she was seeing. She gave a half-turn to go and then it happened.

'Don't.'

Boudicca turned back. She stuck her head out the window and peered around in the ample moonlight to see if someone else was there. 'Who said that?' she whispered.

'I did.'

Boudicca couldn't believe what she was seeing and hearing. 'Finn?'

'Yes.'

'I'm dreaming?'

'You're not dreaming. This is real.'

'Real? Feels unreal to me. I mean you can talk, I'm talking to a hare.'

'Yes,' Finn said. 'What's unreal about that?'

'The fact that I am discussing reality with a talking hare, suggests otherwise!' Boudicca figured that by chatting, sense would pour back into the moment and not allow fantasy, madness or magic to explain it away.

'You must come with us.'

'Us?'

'Yes. The Fia and me.'

'The Fia?'

'The deer,' he said.

The deer nodded slowly, his massive antlers exaggerating the movement.

'Where are we going?'

'The Ullauns. It is important that you come.'

Before she knew it, she was in her slippers, wrapped in her nightgown, standing beside the deer. He lowered his hind to facilitate her climbing onto his back. Boudicca glanced back at the cottage in the moonlight and then looked down to the locket in her hand. She placed it around her neck, pulling her nightgown tightly around her shoulders.

Finn instructed her to grab the mane on the Fia's neck. Cautiously she did as asked and could not speak even if she wished to, fearing that words would somehow break the spell of the moment. On the garden wall sat Maurice Fitzgerald, the cat, disinterestedly looking on.

'Maurice,' said Finn, with a nod, as the group silently trotted past.

The cat licked his paw, paused and then looked away.

'Civil as ever that cat,' Finn said to himself, with a mild shake of his head.

With Finn and Boudicca onboard, the deer set off at a pace, scaling the high garden wall in one bound, moving toward the park and the darkness beyond. A moment later the shadows grew lush, dark and hungry, swallowing them whole.

# Chapter 3

The Book of Merak

*Chapter 779*

*Verse 21*

*On bees collecting*

*It is now between the eleventh and third moon following. The nectar is deep in the flower and pollen collecting on the hip. The colours entrance, there is joy in our work. We are drunk as we return with much winking and smiles between us. The Queen will surely be pleased, yet she will not let us know. But we shall know, because we have collected. We hear the dances of others and where abundance lies. They are drunk too. You can see the flowers, their heads bent and heavy. Heavy heads is what we can see and we Bees plunder as we wish.*

The deer's hooves beat out the rhythm of the run.

Trees followed rocks, rocks followed lakes and lakes followed other trees beneath the animal's broadening stride. Boudicca heard soft grunts come from the deer as it jumped over rivers and fallen trunks, his tongue lolled as he inhaled the cold air and exhaled warmth with languorous ease. She had no idea where she was going, yet did her best to hold onto the animal's mane, hiding behind the protective canopy of his antlers. She kept her exhilaration in check, yet wished at every moment to scream with wild delight. The deer galloped with purpose, knowing the pathless woods and the secrets of unseen rocks.

She found that her deformed foot sat snugly in the thick hair of the animal's flank. A spur on his shoulder bone was the perfect height for a stirrup, his anatomy seemed moulded for her imperfection. After a lifetime of things not fitting, she felt almost complete sitting on the back of this great creation.

After a while, the deer slowed as they approached a hill amongst thick forest. On it, a mighty rounded rock of granite, the width of the hillock and the height of a bus. Boudicca heard the Fia's hooves padding on the moss beneath, moving from a slow trot to a fast walk. The first thing she noticed was the size of the trees, their broad bases were the width of town houses, hulking trunks that tapered off to the sky. It reminded her more of prehistoric vegetation that she had read about in school science projects. There was nothing small here.

'We are here,' Finn said.

'Where is here?' she asked.

'Cumann Rock. I am bringing you to meet your kind.'

'My kind?'

'An Ullaunite is what you are, Boudicca,' Finn said, 'a fact that cannot be changed, an immeasurable power and a heavy responsibility.'

'What sort of power?' Boudicca readjusted herself on the deer's back.

'The power to protect the secrets of Nature, an Ullaunite is a guardian of the very magic at the centre of life. We protect nature and nature protects us.'

Boudicca raised her eyebrows at the confidence and clarity of the hare's response.

'Prospero told you of The Ullauns. It is not a forest measured by the acre but a special place, a manifold world, with many worlds within. Hard to imagine now, but this will soon become clearer.'

'No priests or doctors here?' asked Boudicca, as she looked around.

'No priests or doctors is right,' Finn replied.

They stopped.

'What now?'

'We wait,' Finn said.

Boudicca looked around. Before long, she heard the sound of rustling from nearby trees. The Fia bent down, allowing them both to dismount. Boudicca was unsure in the darkness, a deep apprehension grew in her and she took a small step to be closer to the deer, feeling a measure of reassurance in his size.

'No need to be fearful,' Finn said, standing on a rock to the left of her, looking over a sea of gigantic fern fronds.

Boudicca saw the outline of figures emerge from the shadows, bathed in moonlight and glowing at their edges.

'Boudicca.'

Distracted by the figures, she turned to Finn to ask a question. To her amazement, she saw that he had changed from a hare into a boy. He was a little older than herself, with nut-brown hair and bright eyes. He was dressed in a leather waistcoat, armlets tied at the wrists with fitted leather pants and boots. His hair was cut tight and his jawline strong, complemented by an aquiline nose. There was a mild intensity to his face, but it had a smile on it, which softened its edges.

'A shape shifter?'

'Yes, but I'm still Finn.'

One of the figures stepped forward, an older man, Boudicca thought. In his mouth was a long white smoking pipe clenched between his teeth. The sides of his head were shaved. Long ringlets of grey curls fanned down from his crown, resting on his shoulders. Boudicca was surprised to see his eyes shining out of the darkness with a piercing yellow colour, a black pupil ponding in the middle. The features of his face were lit by tobacco embers as he puffed his pipe.

'Finn,' the man said, with a low voice.

'Tycho, here she is.'

'This is Tycho Asio, another Ullaunite,' Finn said.

Tycho extended his left hand.

Boudicca had to make a conscious effort to shake it, an unusual social convention for her. 'Nice to meet you,' she said. She saw another armlet at his wrist, covered in foliage designs.

Tycho looked to the Fia, and bowed. 'We praise you Fia, for bringing this Ullaunite to us,' he announced, with reverence.

The deer bowed. Then, as quickly as he had arrived, bolted off into the darkness as if startled.

From behind Tycho, came the sounds of fluster and grunts. Boudicca could make out the form of a portly woman, as she laboured her way down from the hill. Plump at every curve, she giggled and chatted to herself while walking. She had the same yellow eyes as Tycho. Her face was open and broad, soft cheek flesh shaking with her every word. A golden tooth shone from her mouth and a golden ring in her nose was attached to a chain, which in turn hung from a ring in her ear. She had leather armlets too, from wrist to elbow like Finn and Tycho. On her waistcoat lapels were pinned a random collection of flowers, twigs, feathers and the skull of a small animal. Boudicca and the lady looked at each other.

'Boudicca?'

'Yes,' Boudicca replied.

The woman smiled. 'My name is Gannymeade Asio, and this is my husband, Tycho Asio.' Gannymeade took in the details of Boudicca's face, her eyes lingering a moment on the girl's forehead. 'Your head must be spinning,' said Gannymeade. 'Firstly, you are under no obligation to stay. Whenever you wish, the Fia will come and take you home. You may eat your fill, drink your sup and think deep on a proposition I have to offer.'

'I will have to be back by breakfast, my grandparents will be getting worried,' said Boudicca, not wishing to make herself too comfortable too quickly.

'I understand, yet time as you know it, is not the same here. A year in the Ullauns can be a moment in your world,' said Gannymeade. Gannymeade beckoned forward those who were behind her. 'You have met Finn Giorra. You will meet the others in time. I don't want to crowd you with too much information and people. All gathered here are like you.'

Boudicca felt somewhat underdressed being in her nightgown and slippers, but little made sense now. 'You mentioned a proposition. What is it?'

'Your mother,' said Gannymeade, looking plainly into her eyes.

'How do you know about her? Is she alive? Do you know where she is?' Boudicca pressed.

'We know your mother. As a girl, she fought with us. An Ullaunite too. She is alive, but is being held against her will.'

Boudicca inhaled the cold night air with relief and worry, in equal measure, besetting her. 'I need to find her and bring her home.'

'You need to know everything before you decide your next

step,' Gannymeade said, gesturing toward the rock.

As she did so, an outline of a rectangular light appeared on the side of the granite monolith. It was a door slightly opened; a warm yellow light diffused from the edges. Boudicca glanced inside and saw a cavernous space, in the middle of which a fire roared.

'But this is a rock?' said Boudicca.

'As I said, you need to know everything before you decide your next step,' repeated Gannymeade. 'I am the Matriarch of the Ullaunite tribe. You may safely leave this place at your pleasing and you will never hear, see or even remember that we ever met, and may you live the rest of your days as such. Or you can follow us and we may have some chance of saving your mother and the Ullauns in which we now stand.' Gannymeade then walked toward the light.

Boudicca stood motionless looking at the gathered figures that formed lines on either side of the door. She placed a hand on her chest, feeling the locket beneath her nightclothes. Not far away she saw the deer with the white stripe emerge from the shadows, ready to bear her off, if she wished. She could have walked to him but was assailed by the thoughts of her mother, so she took a deep breath, looked to the moon and then walked forward, the limp in her slippers obvious to all. Bathed in warm light, the granite door closed softly behind her.

# Chapter 4

The Book of Megrez

*Chapter 93*
*Verse 212*

*On the run of squirrels*

*Here she comes, she spies me and what I have gathered for her in the sixth and seventh moon and she runs, and I run after and joy lightens our hearts and she lets me catch up and my tail is high and she lets me nuzzle her and she does not leave.*

*He spies me and I see what he has gathered for me in the sixth and seventh moon and I run and he runs after and joy lightens our hearts and I let him catch up and his tail is high and I do not leave and he does not leave. It seems we are now one.*

The ceiling within Cumann Rock was so high that Boudicca only saw a weakened form of firelight reach it. As tall as a cathedral, the upper shadows danced and grew spectral amongst its high arches.

Along the walls Boudicca saw an extensive and multi-layered tangle of roots covering all available space. All seemed scorched and singed as if a great fire had taken place. Behind the roots lay a multitude of books, the edges charred, root tips coming out from the wall were blackened. On the wall closest to her, wreathed in the tangle, was a coat of arms cut from stone. A circle of seven stars, at the centre of which stood the image of a leaping salmon, beneath it the words in arch writing, "Somnia Sine Metu". It was Latin. She repeated the words to herself. She knew "Somnia" meant sleep or dream, indicative singular, "Sominate", indicative plural. She also knew "Sine" was the Latin for "without". "Metu" was an unknown to her.

'Dream without fear,' Tycho said, as he showed her to a stool near the fire. She saw a tendril of smoke coming from Gannymeade's pipe who sat considering the girl, the chain jingling as it dangled from her nose and ear like a slack telegraph wire, her eyes less yellow in the warm firelight.

'I am unsettling you with my gaping,' said Gannymeade.

Boudicca shook her head with a calm disregard.

'You remind me of your mother. The high cheeks, those brilliant eyes, the rowdy hair. She's another Sarah,' Gannymeade announced.

Boudicca smiled to herself, happy that her mother was being talked about. "Rowdy" was a word her mum would use too. Boudicca took a breath and reconsidered her intention with solemnity. 'I wish to find my mother.' Her eyes and face became imbued with steely resolution. 'I wish this. With all my heart.'

'And we wish to help you,' said Gannymeade, smoke cascading from the side bar of her mouth.

Boudicca saw Finn, now standing at a height near the roof of the chamber, balancing on one of the roots coming out from the wall. Assured at the great height, he took a book from a shelf, sat on the root and seemed to read. As her eyes became more accustomed to the light, she saw a section of the chamber where volumes of books were stacked in their thousands, reclining in shelves entirely made of roots. Each book seemed to have a root attached to the spine, and as such were arranged in differing sizes and shapes covering the walls. They were dust covered, leatherbound and singed. Boudicca thought them ancient and dormant.

Gannymeade noticed Boudicca's lingering eyes. 'You like books?' she asked.

'Oh yes,' said Boudicca, with enthusiasm, 'yes indeed – as many as I can get my hands on.' Her eyes now taking in the extent of library and the immensity of the volumes. 'How many do you have here?'

'Too many to count. What you see here is the repository of learning. All of nature and the universe reside here.'

Gannymeade gestured with her hand and lights came up on a system of shelves. Closest to them were innumerable pillars entirely made of roots stacked with books as tall as a city high-rise, the spaces in between them were as long as a network of city streets. Every available space on the shelves was packed. Looking left and right Boudicca saw similar pillars and could hardly grasp the immensity of the books present and the space containing them.

'What you are looking at, is the Omnium Gatherum,' puffed Gannymeade, 'the greatest library no one knows about. A library of all that is knowable and unknowable, in nature and beyond. But books lie dormant, and the knowledge within them out of reach. Before you ask why, I will tell you at a later date when you have become more familiar with our ways.'

'Omnium Gatherum,' Boudicca mouthed, delighting in its sound.

At ground level, she noticed corridors branching off into different directions. From the side of the fire, Tycho arrived, bringing a tray on which sat a teapot and a muslin covered plate. Gannymeade gestured with an open hand, offering the teapot and pulling away the muslin cloth to reveal cheese and bread lying on the crockery beneath.

'Juniper tea?' asked Gannymeade.

'Thank you,' Boudicca said, finding herself hungry after the night's journey. She gobbled down all the food as if urged on by a mysterious appetite that seemed to be growing within her. She barely took a breath between mouthfuls – something she would never have done before. She seemed less conscious of herself around the fire in Cumann Rock.

'The fresh air makes you hungry. Not unusual on the first visit. It is called the Famish,' Gannymeade assured, with a smile.

Boudicca slowed her chewing, yet her eyes were quick and alive, looking at all she could, breathing through her nose and munching with her shut mouth, her eyes devouring with equal speed.

'You will not want for food here,' said Gannymeade, nodding to herself and then to the fire.

A silence rested over them a moment.

'What do you think of the tea?' Gannymeade asked, conscientiously, her face red-cheeked from the warmth as light danced along her nose chain.

'Didn't think I'd like it, but tonight has been full of surprises,' Boudicca said, gesturing to the cup in her hand.

'Oh, a magical brew,' said Gannymeade.

Boudicca moved her lips back from the cup, her eyes cautious, a knee jerk nervousness and suspicion coming out in her. 'It won't put me to sleep will it?' she asked.

'No. Tonight is all about awakening for you.'

'Where are we?' Boudicca gently dusted crumbs from her mouth.

'Geophysically, you are in the forest of The Ullauns, not far from your grandparents house. Around us are the Lakes of Killarney, Muckross House and the mountains close by.'

'Geophysically?' Boudicca was puzzled.

'Geophysicals are not important here. The Ullauns is an ancient world. What you see in the Park is merely a gateway, a perforation in space where many worlds lie. A nexus if you will. A crossroads.'

Boudicca recalled the conversation with Prospero earlier.

Gannymeade turned to the fire again, seeking consolation in its warm light, her gaze dancing on flame tips. 'We live in dangerous times Boudicca Moriarty. Nature fights for its very life, and darkness grows stronger.'

'What darkness?' asked Boudicca.

'Mustela. A former Ullaunite who has turned against his own. He has raised an army that vastly outnumbers ours, and wields it under the banner of the Regnum. He wishes to control all of nature for his own end and wipe us out.'

'What type of army?'

'Robusti. A bloodthirsty breed bent on his bidding.'

Boudicca thought a moment. 'You say outnumbers. How many are we talking about?'

'How many books are stacked before your eyes?' replied a saturnine Gannymeade, her gaze unflinching from the fire.

Boudicca looked to the expanse of books on all sides. The numbers were suitably vast. 'And how many Ullaunites are there?' she pressed further.

'Eleven.'

'Eleven?' said a calm, yet disbelieving Boudicca.

'I'm wrong!' Gannymeade looked up from the fire at Boudicca.

'Twelve, if you decide to join us.' She repositioned her rump and stared solidly at the new arrival. 'We are all that's left, the last line of defence. And that line, may I add, is very thin. Finn!' Gannymeade suddenly called, from the side of her mouth.

Finn replaced the book and jumped from a tremendous height, four stories of a building at least. A cloud of dust rose where he landed. Boudicca slowly blinked at the feat, saying nothing yet loudly swallowing the remainder of the dry bread in her mouth.

'Heights aren't a problem then,' smiled Boudicca.

'Heights are the least of our problems,' Gannymeade replied, and then turned to Finn. 'Can you show Boudicca the others. She needs to know all before she decides.'

'What of The Bonding?' asked Finn. 'Will I ready her?'

Gannymeade nodded.

'What is The Bonding?'

'It's a term we use to describe the animal spirit you have inside you. Every Ullaunite has one,' said Gannymeade, picking up a taper, lighting it off an ember and putting to the pipe's cup.

'Don't worry. It's not painful,' Finn reassured. He showed Boudicca a doorway that led to another chamber. As she limped past him, his eyes shot up to Gannymeade, who puffed on in contemplation. The pair left in silence.

'That was a big jump back there,' Boudicca said, after a while of quiet walking.

'More of a hop really.'

'Well you are a hare!'

Finn smiled. 'I am.'

After a while he moved to a connecting hallway, at the end of which was a door, covered in mechanical parts. A collection of sprockets, gears and the jetsam of levers, hanging from nails, wires and springs. Finn knocked on the door.

'Who is it?' enquired a voice, from inside.

'Finn! I have come with Boudicca.'

Tarquin Martes opened the door. He was a boy about the same age as Finn, dressed in identical leathered livery. Finn introduced him.

'Nice to meet you,' Tarquin said, extending his left hand, from which fell a piece of wood that landed at Boudicca's feet. 'Oh how clumsy of me,' he said, and made to pick it up. Boudicca bent down first, as it was closest to her. Taking the wood from her, Tarquin re-presented his left hand and they shook.

'What are you doing?' enquired Finn, as they followed him into an adjoining chamber.

Tarquin pointed to a far-off corner and a number of holes in the ground. 'Some of the badgers from Rattle Pass wish to move their setts to higher ground. The river level is growing. We're discussing digging techniques, and layout.'

Out of the holes appeared the heads of some badgers, their noses dusted from digging.

'Keep going lads, all the way up to the top level,' called Tarquin, to the Badgers. One of them nodded and they returned to their work.

'You're teaching the badgers to dig?' Boudicca asked.

'No, no, they can dig with ease. We're just discussing options.'

Boudicca raised her eyebrows.

Over Tarquin's shoulder lay the open door of an adjoining workshop. Inside stood an older man wearing spectacles with extending lenses cantilevering off his nose, he had a net in his hand and was flustered. His face was lit by the glow of numerous fireflies. Looking bemused, the man put his hands on his hips like a mother chastising wayward children. He whispered energetically to the insects. Boudicca strained to listen but she couldn't hear any words. The fireflies responded by forming an orderly line and returned to a glass jar on the bench. The man replaced the top and leaned on a stool for a moment's rest, dabbing his brow with a handkerchief. 'Almost there,' he announced. 'Sometimes they get so excited, they listen to no one.'

'This is my father,' Tarquin said, 'Old Joe.'

'Fireflies when excited are deaf to orders,' Old Joe said, as he emerged wiping his face and presenting his left hand. His armlets frayed at the edges, covering lean arms, his veins crisscrossing like small rivers on a map. Boudicca noticed Old Joe's eyes were green like Tarquin's and in constant squint, as if in an eternal quandary, pondering the spin of things. Boudicca saw an old man with a kind face, alive with youthful inquisition.

As Boudicca shook his hand, she felt a rush of sudden cold and looked to Old Joe's armlet. There she gazed at the swirling ivy pattern shrink and retreat away to nothing. On it the letter "I" appeared. She thought it strange and glanced into the old man's eyes where she found a disguised vacancy behind their green lightness. She peered down at the armlet. The ivy had returned. The letter "I" had disappeared. All seemed normal again.

'Fireflies.' Boudicca smiled. From the side of her eye, she saw Tarquin looking at her short leg in its slipper.

Old Joe reacted by flicking the back of Tarquin's head. 'Begging your pardon Boudicca,' said Old Joe, in mild censure. 'Someone has forgotten their manners. He means no harm. It's the way his mind works. Like me, he stares sometimes, forever tackling conundrums. Do forgive us, it's our nature.'

Tarquin gathered himself and bowed in apology.

'Tarquin and Old Joe are the inventors,' said Finn, feeling the need to interject.

'We make the returners,' Old Joe said, tapping the wooden knife on his hip. 'Now, Tarquin, those badgers wish to finish and I wish to dust these fireflies. Firefly dust does not gather itself, you know.'

Boudicca smiled at the familial nature between them.

'Nice to meet you again, Boudicca,' said Tarquin, as he returned to the badgers.

Before returning to the workshop Old Joe placed what looked to Boudicca like a tooth into Finn's hand. 'As requested, Finn,' said Old Joe, with a bow.

Finn bowed in reply and walked away, Boudicca didn't enquire any further and briefly wondered if the old man was a dentist as well.

Boudicca and Finn walked down another connected hallway, where roots intertwined above their heads in an arch. This led to a pathway that lowered into a gully, at the bottom of which lay a stream that trickled quietly as if wishing to be ignored. Its soft sound echoed into the cavern. Boudicca moved carefully around roots and over stones.

'We are now in the chamber of the Sciurus,' Finn said.

In the middle of the chamber stood a blonde-haired boy.

'Liam,' whispered Finn.

Liam quietened him with a finger to his mouth and beckoned them to join him closer.

'Liam Sciurus. Boudicca Moriarty,' whispered Finn, introducing Boudicca with a gesture.

Liam smiled and extended his hand.

Boudicca shook hands and looked around at the enormous cavern.

'Liam is our physician,' added Finn.

'A shaman too, don't forget,' said Liam, without looking, his eyes trained on the ceiling above.

Finn smiled. 'A shaman too, forgive me. Where are the others?'

'It's the last run,' said Liam.

'Impressive,' said Finn.

'Yes, these ones are very fast indeed,' said Liam, looking at the network of roots covering the walls and roof.

'What's happening?' Boudicca asked.

'A relay race between my two sisters, Alba and Niamh, and a troupe of red and grey squirrels,' Liam informed her. 'We're teaching the squirrels escape routes and speed of limb.'

'Alba and Niamh are lightning-fast climbers,' said Finn, 'the fastest?'

Liam nodded without looking. 'If you're faster than them, then you're very fast.' Liam smiled in quiet pride. He cleared his throat and called out. 'OK, everyone, this is the last run.'

High up in the ceiling hung two blonde girls amongst the roots. Alba hung by one hand, feet dangling in the air. Niamh sat close by on a root. Boudicca saw no fear of heights in these girls. A red squirrel stood by awaiting the signal.

Liam opened his palm in which sat an acorn seed. 'First one to collect the acorn in my hand is the winner.'

Boudicca was excited at the playful suspense.

'Go!'

Both Alba and the red squirrel, set off at an incredible pace. Alba was easier to see due to her hair and size but Boudicca could see a movement close to her. It was the squirrel. They climbed and scurried through the shadows cast across the walls and roof, as they navigated their way around, swinging and jumping from root to root. At the turn the squirrel claimed the lead, but only just. When a full turn around the roof had been completed, the red squirrel tipped the paw of a grey squirrel and Alba slapped hands with Niamh, the relay had been completed and both took off at a blistering pace.

The competitors made their way off the roof roots and onto the wall, where Niamh had an advantage of size. She soon made up the ground on the squirrel, making huge jumps and landing them without breaking her stride. It was a formidable feat of balance and stamina. Boudicca was instantly amazed by their agility and strength.

At the end of the full circumference, both touched the ground and scampered to retrieve the acorn. Niamh reached her brother first. She was about to pick the acorn from his hand, when he mischievously threw it in the air. Niamh saw it rise. From behind, the grey squirrel appeared on Niamh's back, leaped from her shoulder, catching the acorn mid-air and landing with it in its grip. The squirrel chirped with delight and was joined by his compatriots as they celebrated ecstatically, throwing the acorn to each other, rising some floor dust.

Niamh looked to Liam. 'Now Liam, was that really fair?'

'No, but you had been good taking it easy on them. The win will make them stronger and more confident,' Liam said, as he winked at her.

The squirrels came back and climbed Niamh and Alba as they stood beside Finn and Boudicca. Their fluffy tails lay across the girl's heads and shoulders. They sat there looking at Boudicca, curious as to the stranger. For a moment, Boudicca felt their stares, as if they looked through her, examining the very bones and marrow inside. When she looked away, she noticed both sisters looking at the slipper on her leg.

Finn saw Boudicca's discomfort and called the girls. 'Alba, Niamh. This is Boudicca Moriarty.'

Both stepped forward. They were younger than Boudicca, both with blonde hair cascading down and dominating their features.

'Hi,' they said, in embarrassed unison.

'Hi,' said Boudicca, with a calming smile.

'Do you think we are twins?' asked Alba, the smaller of the two and still a little puffed from her exertions.

'Before you say anything, we're not twins,' said Niamh.

'Even though we look alike, there are a few years between us,' explained Alba.

'How many years do you think?' asked Niamh.

'Oh yes, please guess! Please. Please.'

Boudicca shrugged her shoulders. 'Years?'

'How many?'

'Two years,' Boudicca guessed.

The girls laughed giddily.

'Try two hundred years,' said Alba.

'Two hundred,' replied Boudicca.

'Time is relative, Boudicca,' reassured Finn.

Boudicca delighted in the lightness of this pair and how they didn't seem as serious as the rest. Alba nudged her sister forward with an elbow. After a little to-ing and fro-ing, Niamh walked forward, her ice blue eyes flashing in the half-light.

'Much is said of you Boudicca, and your mother too.'

'What has been said?' Boudicca asked.

'That your mother was a brave Ullaunite, there was great power in her and she helped us in times past. Some say your line goes back to the time of the ancients, to the time of bears. Do you think that's true?' asked Alba.

'I don't know. I am unsure of a lot.'

'Please, not now Alba,' interrupted Finn.

'We need as much help as we can get right now. I would like to think of you as an ancient Ullaunite,' pressed Alba.

'Thank you Alba,' said Finn.

'Me too,' said Niamh.

Alba and Niamh approached Boudicca. Alba gave her a smile and shook Boudicca's hand clumsily. Niamh did the same. They giggled at their own impetuousness.

'Don't mind us,' added Niamh, 'we've got lots of energy.'

Both turned and whispered to the squirrels, then bounded off, leaping to the root walls. Boudicca watched them jump a great distance in one bound and perch on the roof again.

'Now that's a jump,' said Finn, to Boudicca.

Liam bade farewell to Boudicca and called out to his sisters, 'We have a flock of wrens arriving for nest building, so this is definitely the last run.'

Boudicca left the chamber smiling. As she left, she couldn't help look over her shoulder at the girls once more, wondering about their knowledge and how they seemed to help nature to adapt and change.

'They're a funny bunch,' Finn said, noticing Boudicca's reaction.

'What if they are right?'

'About what?'

'That I am an ancient Ullaunite. What does that mean?'

'No one or no thing can tell, only time,' Finn replied. 'It's best not to think of such things. You have to trust nature and the magic around it. This will let you and us know soon enough what you are.'

They walked along a more intricate labyrinth of intersecting hallways, entering another chamber. After a moment of silence Finn stopped, Boudicca saw a girl in the middle of the chamber, her skin a black colour. Her hair white and spiked, long at the back and plaited on some lengths all the way down to her waist, dressed also in the familiar leathers. All that could be heard was the sound of a soft clicking.

'Constantina Pipistrelle,' said Finn, in a hushed tone.

On the girl's arm stood five swallows looking at her intently and then to the floor. Standing at differing spots from the shoulder to the little finger, they seemed to be listening to whispered instructions. She was showing them a map drawn on the dusted floor, with topographical features – mountains and valleys – rising out and dug deep in relief.

'What is she doing?' asked Boudicca.

'Showing them the way home,' replied Finn.

Boudicca moved to a taller stone to get a better look at the map. She could see Constantina take the swallows through their migratory journey from their summer breeding grounds in Kerry. Walking slowly as she whispered and clicked her tongue to the birds, their wings fluttered with anticipation as they travelled across the ocean on the floor, through western France, over the Pyrenees, a cluster of rocks, down eastern Spain into Morocco and across the Sahara. The journey would take place at the end of July. Then Boudicca saw Constantina show them an alternate route that followed the coast of Africa avoiding the Sahara by travelling further east and down the Nile Valley. All the time she clicked and whispered to the swallows that were perched in rapt attention.

Finn tapped Boudicca on the shoulder and pointed to the other side of the cavern. Ithaca, her brother, stood alone. His face was a deep black colour too, his hair was white and spiked, with a mullet growing down to the hip. No light seemed to escape from his skin, except for the brilliance of his teeth as he spoke with excitement into his cupped hands. In front of him sat three wooden buckets. Opening his hands, Boudicca could just make out a solitary bee standing there. Ithaca placed a moon daisy beneath the bucket on the right-hand side. He whispered to the bee, which took off, leaving his hand and the chamber.

'What is he doing?' asked Boudicca, looking on in puzzlement.

'Telling the bee where the flower is.'

'But the bee can see that.'

'Ah, but the challenge is whether the bee can communicate that information to the others,' explained Finn.

Moments later Boudicca heard a low drone coming from a corridor. It was the sound of the hive as they made their way back, searching for the moon daisy. They arrived in their thousands, a mass of buzzing energy, the swarm staying together in the air, reviewing the three wooden buckets. All descending on the correct bucket, which quickly became a buzzing ball of contentment. The bees turned the bucket over and through collective industry and cooperation, brought the daisy to the top of the ball.

Ithaca picked the flower with nimble fingers, not wishing to get stung. He whispered and clicked to the ball of bees who immediately dispersed, making their exit out a hole in the wall. Boudicca was speechless in wonder having never before seen such communicative connection between human and insect, and in such a clear and calm manner too. The swallows also left Constantina's arm, following the bees at a safe distance.

Finn interrupted Boudicca's thoughts. 'I have someone for you to meet.'

As the pair made their way closer, Boudicca noticed they were clicking their tongues with their eyes shut.

'Tell me why their eyes are closed?' Boudicca said.

'It doesn't matter if their eyes are open or closed,' Finn replied. 'Why?'

'Because we are blind,' interjected Constantina, with a crisp clarity.

As Finn introduced the Pipistrelle siblings, Boudicca noticed that both moved their heads from side-to-side as they clicked.

'We click to echolocate,' began Constantina.

'Like bats,' ventured Boudicca.

'Exactly. We can see things in detail but without colour,' said Ithaca.

'May we feel your face?' asked Constantina.

'There is only so much we can see with our clicking. Sometimes our hands aid our eyes,' reassured Ithaca.

Boudicca looked to Finn hesitantly, but he nodded in encouragement.

'Alright,' said Boudicca.

Constantina was first to move forward, gliding her fingers gently over Boudicca's face, checking the contours of her eyes and nose.

'Where are you from?' asked Constantina, wishing to put Boudicca at ease.

'Oxford,' Boudicca replied.

Constantina stopped, her thumbs resting on the closed lids of Boudicca's eyes. She found Ithaca's hand – who was more focussed on her ears and forehead – and placed them on Boudicca's face.

'Her brow!' said Ithaca, smiling.

'What about it?' asked Boudicca, worriedly.

'It's very strong. Those related to the ancients have strong brows,' reassured Constantina, who was feeling Boudicca's hands and then moving down her longer leg. 'You may think this very presumptuous of us,' Constantina added, 'but doing this helps us immensely, because when … when, we … we … we …' Constantina stopped.

'What is it?' asked Boudicca.

She began to click, now feeling the muscular rigidity of Boudicca's shorter leg. She could feel the scarring from the operations.

'My leg,' said Boudicca.

'This is a source of great pain for you.'

Boudicca didn't reply.

'Where there is pain, there is strength,' said Constantina.

Boudicca stepped back. 'Sometimes, I'd rather be normal than strong,' she replied.

'We are sorry if we have offended,' Ithaca said, his head lowered.

'Yes,' reiterated Constantina, 'we did not mean to offend.'

'I'm fine,' said Boudicca. 'It's just the way it is, isn't it.'

'We bid you welcome,' said Constantina.

Both walked away clicking, as they returned to their work.

Finn led Boudicca to another chamber a little further on. Seats made from roots edged a low fire. They sat in silence for a moment.

'It is my job to tell you of the dangers,' began Finn, clearing his throat.

Boudicca composed herself.

'We are locked in a battle with the Regnum. Their leader is Mustela. He wishes to have the power that comes from our Anam. The Anam is our soul, that soul is connected to the soul of nature. That soul can be extracted in the form of an oil. The Regnum needs our oil to thrive and they have found a way … to extract our souls.'

'Extract?' asked Boudicca, puzzled.

'They hunt us to defeat us, but also to harvest us. Our Anam is extracted, which they then use to make themselves bigger and stronger. Mustela has a Praetorian guard called Decima, who is as dark and powerful as she is dangerous.'

Boudicca sat riveted.

'They search, too, for the Children of Bears.'

'The Children of … Bears?' asked Boudicca.

'Seven books containing all the secrets of The Ullauns and thus nature. Seven books given to us by the Ancients. Immensely powerful. They were last seen on the night of Harrows. Each book is named after a star in the Ursa Major constellation, in the night sky. Alkaid, Mizar, Alioth, Phad, Merak, Dubhe and …'

'Megrez,' said Boudicca, finishing his sentence.

'Indeed,' said Finn, smiling.

Boudicca suddenly remembered the image from the wall of Cumann Rock.

'Like the seven stars in the coat of arms,' she said.

'Very observant.'

Boudicca put her hand to her chest and felt the locket against her skin. She shivered and pulled her dressing gown tightly around her neck.

'Are you cold?' Finn asked.

'No I'm fine,' said Boudicca, with a light shake of her head.

'These books contain the secrets of Nature's power. They tell its stories. Why flowers grow? Why foxes hunt? Why bees collect nectar? The why of things?'

Boudicca nodded.

'In desperate times, people look for a saviour, someone to turn the tide,' said Finn.

'That's why they look at me.'

'Yes. Our folklore has it that a creature called Ursine, a being who will come and return the child of bears. The books of nature that have been lost for generations. That being will come and help us.'

'They thought I was going to be this saviour. But they don't believe it, do they? Not with this … leg of mine.'

Finn smiled. 'They're careful who they believe in and what they believe in. Don't scold them for that. We need all the Ullaunites we can gather right now!'

Boudicca appreciated Finn's straight talking.

Finn inhaled deeply and looked into the dark edges of the cavern. 'It's not a dream Boudicca. A final reckoning will soon be upon us. I need you to know that you could die here.'

His words rested heavily with her. 'What would happen, if I did?'

'In your world, you would just go missing. A mystery that others would never solve.'

She paused.

'Are you saying this Mustela has taken my mother?'

'Yes.'

Boudicca was quiet for a moment.

'There is only one thing left to do, if you wish to join us.'

'What's that?'

'The Bonding.'

'What, now?'

'As good a time as any.'

Boudicca looked to the fire and nodded.

The Ullaunites gathered in the firelight of Cumann Rock. Finn led Boudicca into the middle where two stools and a table stood; on the table was a lighting candle.

Gannymeade joined them. They both sat opposite each other.

'No need to be nervous Boudicca, the Bonding is just a way to find what animal you have in your nature. Every Ullaunite has a connection to the animal kingdom, and as such, this is a retracing of your lineage. It is painless and you will be awake the whole time.'

Boudicca nodded at the reassurance.

'What we are about to do is go to a place in your mind called the Pivot where your animal will be revealed to me,' Gannymeade said. 'There are no good or bad animals, just the bond. At any time you can stop me by saying, stop.'

Boudicca nodded.

Gannymeade placed her hands on the table, palms facing up. 'Now, put your hands on mine and then focus on the candle flame in front of you.'

Boudicca did as requested.

Gannymeade closed her eyes and for the briefest of moments, hardly a blink of the eye. 'You are a deer Boudicca. A very powerful animal.'

Gannymeade smiled, yet Boudicca felt somewhat underwhelmed by the experience. The others gathered and gave a brief round of applause. She seemed happy with the outcome, as she always liked the deer in the Park and felt a natural bond with them. 'What happened when you closed your eyes?'

'As I have done before with all the rest,' said Gannymeade, 'I wait in front of a mighty cave, the inside of which is completely dark. I wait and the animal that comes out into the light is your animal.'

Boudicca nodded.

'A young fawn emerged from the cave for you,' said Gannymeade, smiling. She invited the others to share Boudicca's special moment – which they did, shaking her hand in congratulations.

After they'd left the chamber, Tycho exchanged a look with Gannymeade.

'Are you ok?' he asked.

'Yes.'

'A fawn emerged?' asked Tycho.

'Yes, a fawn. But I sensed something else in the cave. Something I couldn't see.'

'Another animal?'

Gannymeade nodded, her eyes widening.

'It slept.'

'A stag maybe?' offered Tycho, with a side look.

'No,' said Gannymeade, 'I heard it snore. Whatever it was, it slept … and it was big.'

Both looked to each other in silence.

'Very big.'

# Chapter 5

The Book of Mizar

*Chapter 581*

*Verse 63*

*On starlings in murmuration*

*We are all eyes and one eye, seeing all and all see us. Through the air we move, ripples on water in thousands of one. And I am at the edge and a move makes me crack like whips end, and we roll on, copying the wind's language. We dance to echo music, the accents of the Boreals are in our sway, envious flocks look on from branches and railings and wish they could join us. All this happens in the evening of the second high moon.*

'A fawn?' Boudicca thought to herself. It suggested youth and innocence but also lack of readiness and potential. Right now she needed to find her mother and did not wish to wait. It was these thoughts that occupied her for much of the night.

A while later, Tycho requested Boudicca to join Gannymeade in one of the rooms off the main chamber. Entering, she found a spartanly furnished room – a table, loose chairs and a potbellied stove, beside which sat Gannymeade, puffing her pipe and kindly regarding the child.

'Finn has told you about what lies ahead.'

Boudicca nodded.

'You will join us?' asked Gannymeade.

'I will do anything, if it helps find my mother.'

Gannymeade sensed Boudicca's sincerity and pointed to the back of the door.

Hanging there was Ullaunite livery. It was made of soft brown leather – waistcoat and armlets, a white shirt, trousers and a jacket. Boudicca moved forward slowly, drawing her fingers across the stitching.

'An Ullaunite is nothing without her armour,' said a smiling Gannymeade. 'See how it fits, then ready yourself – the group will leave soon.'

'Where are we going?' asked Boudicca.

'Collecting the wild seed of the Ullauns,' added Gannymeade, who had already left the room, the door closing behind her.

Moments later Boudicca emerged from Cumann Rock, hesitant and sheepish in her new attire. She was still wearing her slippers, yet all nodded in agreement thinking her well suited to her new uniform. The locket still hung around her neck beneath her shirt.

'Quite the transformation,' observed Tarquin Martes.

'Suits you very well Boudicca,' Niamh said.

Finn called Niamh and Alba forward. The Sciurus girls came with a pair of returners in their hands, which they presented to Boudicca with a ceremonial bow. Boudicca took them, admiring their ornately designed hilts. The leather scabbards were embossed with swirls along the edge, in the centre stood a deer rampant.

'These are your returners. Made of sheoak. An extension of yourself and part of your being,' said Gannymeade. 'None shall control them other than you. They will comfort you and serve you all the days of your life.'

Finn joined in, further rallying the group. 'All of us are bound together through nature. We swear to protect it at all costs. Avoid fighting where you can, engage where you must.'

'Somnia Sine Metu,' he called.

'Somnia Sine Metu,' came the reply, returners unsheathed and pointed to the moon above.

Having never put on a returner before, Boudicca was having trouble tying the straps.

Tarquin stepped in. 'May I?' He offered to reposition her sheaths so that they sat more comfortable on her hips. 'I made them for you,' added Tarquin, 'they can hear you, feel you, think with you. They wish to obey your command. It's not just a sword, it is many things in one.'

'How is this possible?' asked Boudicca.

'It's the wood you picked up,' said Tarquin. 'Sheoak, can accept a spirit with one touch.'

She inspected her returners and noticed their keenness. 'I've never held a weapon before,' said Boudicca, with mild trepidation.

'Don't think of it as a weapon. Think of it as a part of you,' Tarquin replied.

'It's just wood though,' said Boudicca, incredulously.

Tarquin smiled. He quickly picked a granite rock – about the size of a loaf of bread – from the ground beside him. Holding it in his hand, he drew the blade across the rock and cleaved it in half. 'Wood can be sharp,' said Tarquin, with a wink.

'I see,' said a surprised Boudicca.

'Just aim and imagine the sword flying from your hand. Once your will has been done, it will return and sit in your palm.'

Boudicca felt the weight of the returner.

'See the cracked branch over there?' said Tarquin, pointing to a dead limb hanging on a far-off tree. 'In your own time, imagine it slicing the branch. Then throw.'

Boudicca closed her eyes. With a good swing of her shoulders, she threw the returner. It spun through the air making a sound that grew dim as it trailed away. To Boudicca's delight, it cut the broken branch. She'd never been so accurate with a throw before and was thrilled at the potency of the weapon.

'You need to be brave when it returns,' said Liam Sciurus. 'Hold that thought in your head.'

'Believe now, Boudicca,' said Tarquin. 'Believe it will do your bidding.'

It then dawned on Boudicca that a returner spinning back at speed was a far more daunting prospect than one leaving. Fearing her hand would be cut off, she tried to be brave, but the sound and the speed unnerved her. As the blade sliced through the air, she grew fearful and pulled her hand away at the last moment. The returner spun past and away into the distance.

'Do not worry,' said Tarquin, 'the sword will fly, until it finds your hand. It wants to be with you.'

Not wishing to fail publicly again, Boudicca put her hand in the air and urged the blade to return. Hearing it whistle from the dark, she focused on holding her nerve. The blade appeared from the shadows. Boudicca steeled herself. Miraculously it stopped an inch from her hand, moving its hilt snugly into her palm. She smiled and now understood what Tarquin meant.

'Well done,' he said.

Liam, Niamh and Alba applauded, nodding to the others.

'See,' Alba and Niamh chorused, 'we knew you could do it.'

Boudicca looked to the returner again. 'You have a gift,' Boudicca said, to Tarquin, sheathing the returner and following the group.

Gannymeade cut short the revelry and placed her hands on Boudicca's shoulders. 'This is where I leave you child. Finn, Ashket and Tarquin will travel with you. The rest will be on outposts, protecting your return journey. Avoid fighting where you can, engage where you must. Somnia Sine Metu.'

'Somnia Sine Metu,' the group replied.

It was the low sound of hooves in the distance, the pounding of a herd on the move. A thundering rhythm echoed through the wood. Out of the darkness, the deer herd arrived. Boudicca's deer, with the familiar white stripe on his forehead, made his way to her. On the back of one of the leading deer was a young girl, ten or so years old at the most. She sat proudly on the animal. There was a strength in her, brown wild hair, alert eyes that shone out in the moonlight, her chin jutting out and taking her time to look at Boudicca, a considered irreverence in her gaze.

'Is this her?' asked the child, on the Fia's back.

'Oh yes,' said Finn, 'let me introduce my sister, Ashket Giorra.'

'She looks petrified,' said Ashket, with a playful smile, and then added, 'I would be too if I were you.' Ashket Giorra expertly leaned off the animal, extending her left and shook Boudicca's while giving her a playful wink. 'Don't worry, I'll take care of you Boudicca.'

'I may need it.' Boudicca nodded doing her best to calm her beating heart.

The others mounted their Fia effortlessly. Boudicca gratefully accepted the assistance of Constantina, who cupped her heel.

'Thank you,' said Boudicca.

Constantina clicked and smiled.

The hooves churned the woodland floor as trees sped past in a blur. After what seemed like a short time, they stopped and alighted – some with greater ease than others.

'What do we do now?' whispered Boudicca, to Ashket.

'We collect the seeds of these trees and wild flowers in the Muan.'

'The Muan?'

'This part of the Ullauns is called Muan. The seeds ensure the future of the forest and of Nature herself, and our Anam,' said Ashket. 'Most are replanted, some are sacrificed in the fire of the mighty salmon – the Bradán.'

Boudicca didn't enquire further, doing her best to stay alert to what was happening around her. She bent down and joined the others as they began picking seeds and saplings on the forest floor. Finn Giorra lifted his head checking for Regnum forces, his eyes scanning trees, his ears keenly listening to the sounds of the forest.

'Be quick, be quick!' he said. 'Quick as you can. Robusti could be near.'

They all worked in close proximity to one other with a quiet and attentive industry. Boudicca looked on, learning, and trying to copy the others. Ashket showed her what to pick and what to leave behind. While looking at Tarquin, Finn and his sister filling their haversacks, Boudicca noticed each of their armlets bore the design and pattern of their time in the Ullauns – their spirit animal. Boudicca inspected her own armlet. She had nothing on hers as yet.

'Don't worry – the designs on your armlets will grow with your time here,' reassured Ashket.

Finn's sister was wise, yet was still a little skittish, young enough to marvel at the danger of these journeys. She wished to tell Boudicca everything she knew as quickly as she could and Boudicca was happy to listen.

'I will tell you of the Robusti, so that in doing so, I may sharpen my own desire to slay them,' she said.

Finn sighed as he could hear Ashket and knew the trouble in trying to silence her when she became animated.

'Robusti are the foulest beings of the Ullauns. There's thuggery in their blood, fracas and fury in every joint. As tall as a man, as strong as hundreds, their bodies are covered in hair, growing to the neckline and forehead. They have fangs. More like swords!'

'Nobody mentioned that,' said Boudicca

'That was silly of them, for the fangs can grow big ... as big as elephant's tusks.'

Boudicca's eyes widened at the news. Tarquin raised his head to reassure her.

'You will be protected from those fangs.'

'Thank you,' smiled Boudicca, even though Tarquin's reassurance seemed cold comfort.

Ashket drew breath before continuing her story. 'All Robusti have the ability to reproduce their own young, who grow within a marsupial pouch. They are called Mungs. They are flung to the ground when they prove too heavy to carry. Robusti serve the Regnum and are under the control of a Lictor, an officer. They live by their creed, "Divide et Impera ... Divide and rule".'

'Shhhh,' said Finn, urging Ashket to focus.

Ashket growled as she let herself be drawn into her own story. After a moment she looked over her shoulder to Finn and saw he was not looking. She continued. 'They destroy nature and hunt us because we protect it – and for our oil.'

Boudicca picked up what she thought was a seed. 'Seed?'

'No,' said Ashket. 'Stone.'

Boudicca nodded and dropped it.

'What of Mustela?' Boudicca asked.

'Mustela is in his lair, deep inside Mount Bolcawn – an old volcano, north of here. There he extracts the Anam oil from Ullaunites.' Ashket stopped collecting for a moment. 'No one really knows about the extraction, as no one caught has ever returned.' Ashket returned to her topic. 'Mustela is surrounded by his forces. He is guarded by a Praetorian, called Decima, who is a creature different to the others and infused with a dark magic. Heed my words, Boudicca Moriarty, if you ever face her, do not engage her. Use your energy to run and hide, for she is immensely strong and exceedingly dangerous.'

Tarquin nodded, seconding Ashket's advice.

'What Lictor do you wish to engage, Ashket?' asked Tarquin.

'Why, Olor, of course,' she said. 'He is not like the others. It is said he is a grafter, once human, then made into a Lictor. He is a clever one, he likes setting traps, but then, so do I.'

A light wind blew across the treetops. Tarquin felt a shudder with the sway of the trees. He looked to the canopy above their heads, noticing the moon struggling to disrobe a cloud.

'What is it, Tarquin?' asked Finn. 'Did you hear something?'

'No,' replied Tarquin, 'that is what's unnerving me.' He felt on edge collecting seed. Tarquin's normal responsibilities were that of an engineer of armaments and tools. Give him a problem and he delighted in finding a solution, but all Ullaunites had to attend the harvesting and Tarquin did as expected.

'Don't worry, Tarquin,' said Ashket, tapping her hip, 'my returners will protect you.'

'Quiet, Ashket,' said Finn.

Tarquin had hardly begun to pick again, when he heard the distinct creak of a pine tree moving in the wind. Finn heard it too and also rose. They saw one of the pine trees nearest them begin to bend and fall to the ground. Finn could see dark figures at the base of the tree, pushing it over.

'Robusti,' Finn called, taking out his returner.

'Yes,' whispered Ashket, inflating her chest and unsheathing her weapon, 'they will feel my returner.'

Boudicca saw pine tree after pine tree crash down with thunderous claps, roots snapping and belching up from the ground. The trees were pushed over by massive force and precision, from different angles by figures unseen. As the trees fell, it became obvious that there was forethought and engineering in the attack. The trees formed a superstructure, splitting the group in two. Finn and Tarquin on one side, Boudicca and Ashket on the other.

'Tarquin, call the Fia!' Finn shouted, spinning the returner in his hand.

Even the Robusti knew not to engage an Ullaunite, unless it was in open space and the numbers were massively in their favour. Though small, Ullaunites, were masters of the dark arts of nature. Tactically the Robusti would wish to separate the youngest – or least experienced – and with overwhelming numbers, their chances would be fancied. It was clear they had earmarked Ashket and Boudicca.

'Boudicca go to Finn,' ordered Ashket, recognising the ploy.

'But you will be ....'

'Go!'

Boudicca made her terrified way through the falling trees. Her limp pained her now, her heart thumping in her chest. She dodged trunks and limbs as best as she could, and soon found herself close to Finn who pulled her closer with his hand.

Robusti emerged in great numbers from the shadows, bounding forward on all fours along the shafts of the fallen trees, their eyes wide, baring their teeth. They had been waiting, ordered to hold until a signal was given. Their superior numbers, at least a thousand to one, made Boudicca blanch with fear. Ashket was now completely surrounded. She looked at the gathering Robusti and took off her haversack, which was filled with seed.

'Finn, ... catch!' she called, throwing the haversack high over the gathered Robusti. It landed in Finn's arms.

'No!' called her brother, his sister's intentions now dawning on him.

'If you want me, you have to catch me!' Ashket announced, to the Robusti. With returner in hand, she turned and ran.

'Do not engage them. Run, Ashket! Run. Escape! You hear?' Finn yelled after her.

A cohort stayed to keep Tarquin, Boudicca and Finn occupied. Another excited patrol went in pursuit of the young Ullaunite. As they chased, some Robusti could not help themselves springing forward, wanting to bring Ashket down. Each time a Robustus sprang, Ashket's preternatural anticipation sensed it. She turned in mid-air, kicked, punched and slashed her attackers, landing soundly on unfamiliar ground without breaking her stride. Her speed and accuracy were now heightened. Boudicca was amazed already by what she had seen from the youngster.

'I have to help her,' Finn said, to Tarquin, 'she is yet too young.'

Tarquin nodded. Finn scaled the pines and fought his way out, following the mob. As the chasing pack tired, a new pack replaced them. They were driving Ashket further into unfamiliar parts of the Ullauns, deeper into Robusti territory.

Rocks and spears were being thrown from a height by those in wait, but Ashket bobbed and weaved to avoid them. She threw her returner in an arc, the blade spinning around in a deadly singing elliptic. Some twenty or more Robusti fell lifeless from the trees, their throats slit. Her returner was eager to serve, returning to her hand as Ashket jumped and cleaved another Robustus upon landing.

The young Ullaunite weaved over the undergrowth, scaling old branches, in an unbroken stride. The Robusti were clumsy and laborious on the forest floor. From a high vantage point, Ashket could see their numbers swelling. There was more strength in their mobs, more prodigious with their Mungs. All Ullaunites were aware that, once separated, they were on their own. Ashket knew it was the consequence of her tribe in a constant state of war.

From the trees, Ashket came to the top of a rock ledge, a low-lying miasma collected amongst the trees below. Catching her breath, she heard their grunting from behind her.

'Anam, Anam, Anam,' they barked.

Ashket moved her finger across her leather armlet and the touch calmed her. Embossed there was the Ullaunite motto. Somnia Sine Metu. She whispered it to herself. She was unable to outrun them any longer and so decided to stand and engage, thinking that she only needed a small victory, to give her time to move, catch her breath and rethink her position.

Ashket made her way to a clearing below, where young pines stood sentry at the edge, pine needles covering the floor. She could hear the wind whistle through the older parent trees and standing in the middle, she raised her arms, pointing her fingers to the moon and then slowly to the tops of two young pines. Closing her eyes, she slowly moved her arms downward, and with a magical force bent the pines toward the ground. The tops of each touched each other behind her back.

Bending her arms back, she pushed the pines in opposite directions creating two tightened springs, a yard above the ground, out of sight, primed and ready to fire. Beads of sweat mushroomed on her brow. She was under pressure with her control of forces holding the trees in position, she was still young and her strength yet to reach its full potential.

The Robusti finally came with their cackling and barking. They delighted in the view of their prey. She appeared to be broken, trapped and frightened. Their mouths were open as they inched forward, hundreds on all sides, carefully picking their steps. Ashket waited for the greatest number of Robusti to come within range. She held her position and trembled lightly. They thought her to be shaking with fear.

'She shakes,' one cackled.

As they said this, Ashket launched herself skyward. Slackjawed, the Robusti watched her soar and drop her arms. The two pines swished out from the sides, sweeping all before them. They cut swathes through a pasture of Robusti, sending them flying in different directions. The trees rocked back to their original standing, the bend having no affect on their sappy pliability. A mob had been wiped out in an instant.

Ashket softly returned to the forest floor, the soles of her feet landing without a sound. Gathering her breath, while delighting in her ingenuity, she heard her name being called. There was silence for a moment, eddies of mist filling the space again.

'Ashket?'

It was Finn. She could see a figure move in the shadows.

''You are safe. What a brave Ullaunite you are,' he cooed.

'Finn, you shouldn't have followed me,' Ashket replied, reprimanding her brother's bloody-mindedness.

'Here comes a Fia,' he said. 'Follow me.'

'Where are you?' called Ashket, peering through the mist. The figure appeared.

Thinner and more angular than Finn, she sensed who it was. 'Olor.'

Ashket squinted and cocked her head now realising her situation. Olor's face was clean, more spectral than a Robustus, more human than Lictor. He was dressed in an unique style – a long black leather coat, collar turned up, buckled at the belly and chest. His ears were an extension of his jaw line, they sat on the side of his head with the effect of tightening the skin on his face. He peered at her from beneath his eyebrows. She barely had time to turn before another pine swished forward. It, too, had been pulled down and spring-loaded, lashed tight with ivy. The tree caught the side of Ashket's head, hurtling her against the rock and knocking her unconscious.

Olor looked on calmly. The hunt was over.

From the bushes an errant Robustus seized his opportunity to attack the unconscious prey, jumping forward and landing on foot and knuckle. One of his canines was black, giving him the name 'Blacktooth.' He crouched over the girl, saliva dripping from his open gob. Olor jumped from the shadows and landed with a kick as Blacktooth reared up on the girl.

'Desist cur! This Ullaunite is mine.'

Blacktooth grovelled, returning to knuckle and foot, with his head and neck slavishly rubbing against Olor's boot. He dared not flash his eyes to his Lictor.

'Apologies, Apologies.'

Olor picked up Ashket with one arm.

'Divide et Impera,' said Blacktooth.

'Divide et Impera,' replied Olor. With those words Olor sped off to Mount Bolcawn eager to present his Ullanite prize.

When Finn arrived at the scene, he knew his sister had been taken. Seeing a bloodstain on the ground, he touched it with his fingers and his eyes grew heavy. Reluctant to leave, he knew there was nothing left here, nothing even to mourn. A deer had bravely followed him through the pines and waited to take him to Cumann Rock. Finn climbed onto the deer's back, looked over his shoulder at the space where his sister was taken and was gone.

·        ✢        ·

Tarquin shared the story to all upon returning to Cumann Rock. The rest listened in shock and fear, mourning their dwindling numbers. Boudicca sat to the side, silently traumatised by what she had witnessed too.

'We need as many Ullaunites as we can muster. She will not have gone far,' argued Finn, his energy fuelled by anger and grief.

The older ones looked at Finn with sympathy. The others lowered their heads.

'She has been taken, Finn,' said Tycho.

'What's your point?'

'He will extract her immediately,' said Liam.

'Maybe, maybe not.' Finn's hard face visibly emotional under the weight of reality.

'It is certain, Finn,' reaffirmed Liam.

Finn didn't wish to listen. 'Do not lower your heads,' he said, 'it vexes me. Do not lower your heads, she is not dead!'

All remained silent.

Finn slowed a little, finding rest for his eyes in the fire. 'We have to get her back, Gannymeade' he implored, without looking.

'Finn,' she started, pathos in her voice.

He knew its meaning and so rose. Angrily, he shook his head and left the chamber.

'Why can't we help her?' asked Alba, after a moment.

'Our numbers are too small,' Gannymeade puffed. 'The loss of one Ullaunite in the pursuit of another would quickly spell the end. Mustela is clever. He would use Ashket as bait and we could be wiped out in one stroke. I am trying to prevent this.'

Boudicca was finding it hard to concentrate, the terror of the Robusti still with her. Her hands trembled. She tried making them into fists, this didn't stop the tremors. She stood up quickly and announced, 'I need to go home.'

'You too? Why?' asked Alba.

Boudicca pressed the locket against her chest. 'Because I'm not sure if I'm in a dream or not. I suspect I'm not. And there are creatures as big as gorillas that want to eat me and all I have is a piece of wood to protect me. And then there's magic. That's new to me, too. I'm too scared to catch my returner, too frightened to walk in the Ullauns, too nervous to rest. I'm just frightened out of my life,' said Boudicca, looking around.

They understood. Gannymeade was first to calm her.

'Of course. There is a Fia outside to take you home.'

Boudicca couldn't look to the others, feeling a deep shame of those who wish to be braver but cannot. She was helpless. 'I'm sorry. I thought I could help you but ....'

No one spoke as she left.

Outside the Fia with the white stripe was waiting and Boudicca climbed him, holding tight the mane. Gannymeade followed on foot behind.

'If you wish, I can rid you of any memory of this. You won't remember a thing.'

From the back of the Fia, Boudicca found the words that had

earlier eluded her. 'Gannymeade, I have a mother who has been kidnapped. I am swamped, trying my best to understand things. Regnums, Lictors, people who race squirrels, seven stars! I ask you, don't take my memory. Take my fear.'

Gannymeade's face changed and she looked to the ground. 'I cannot,' she said. 'Like everyone else, fear is your concern.'

'I'm sorry then.' Boudicca lingered with a look, and then spurred the Fia to bolt, taking her towards home.

A moment later, Boudicca was standing on Nonie's lawn at the open window of her bedroom in her dressing gown and slippers. Her fia was gone. A blue dawn tinged the sky and would soon be here. Climbing in the window, she lay in her bed and was asleep in an instant.

On the garden wall, Maurice Fitzgerald had a still warm wren beneath his paw. He sat there considering whether or not to take it into Prospero and Nonie as a present – or just leave it on the wall out of pure carelessness.

# Chapter 6

The Book of Dubhe

*Chapter 338*
*Verse 7*

*On a deer's rut.*

*I am immortal, greater than gods who claim to have made me. Anything less is an insult. My chest burns and blooms, ten hearts within. My antlers are mighty and pointed with intent. I eye-ball every other male, picking the serious and desperate and avoid the others. I am full now, alive now and dare now, and some take me on and they will be defeated.*

*I am immortal, greater than gods who claim to have made me.*

'Wake up, child. Wake up, Boudicca. There are people here to meet you.'

Boudicca stirred at the sound of her name being called. It was Nonie at her bedroom door. Boudicca wiped the sleep from her eyes and sat up straight. Close by, she saw her slippers and dressing gown. She felt the locket still on her chest. Picking up her gown, she put it to her nose, thinking there would be the smell of her night's travels. It smelled, however, of her home in Oxford and nothing else. She checked her slippers. They, too, had no trace of her midnight adventure. She wondered if it was the most vivid dream she'd ever had.

Dressed now, she moved down the hall, calling ahead for Finn. Nonie met her half-way, shaking her head.

'He's not here. Wild come, wild go,' said Nonie, straightening Boudicca's shirt.

'Who's in the Kitchen?' asked Boudicca, warily.

'The Guards ... sorry, the police,' said Nonie, with puckered lips.

Boudicca froze, not wanting to take another step. Her feet felt as if nailed to the floorboards for fear of bad news. However, she willed herself forward in the hope of news of a more encouraging kind.

At the table sat a female Irish police officer in uniform – hair in a bun, hat on the table. Her skin was pale and freckled. The man beside her wore smart plain clothes. His skin more sallow – thin and well-groomed – like the member of a tennis club, Boudicca thought.

Prospero poured tea abundantly into china cups. 'This is Garda Hickey, from the station in Killarney,' he said, of the smiling female officer. 'And this is Chief Inspector Jones, from the Thames Valley police in England.'

The man got to his feet and nodded.

'Hello. Have you found her?' Boudicca asked.

'Not yet,' replied C I Jones, 'but rest assured we are still looking.'

Prospero and Nonie glanced across the table. Boudicca nodded impassively.

'We would like to talk to you,' said Garda Hickey. 'Is that ok?'

Boudicca flashed her eyes at the officer.

'I know you have talked to other officers,' CI Jones said, 'and we are not here to interview you. We just want to see if you can think of anything – anything at all – that may have come to mind since visiting your family.'

Boudicca pictured him practising a tennis serve. 'Like what?' she asked.

'Like something you may have remembered perhaps?' said CI Jones.

'Has anything unusual happened since you arrived?' intervened Garda Hickey, confident in the ice-breaking abilities of her puppy-eyed smile.

However, Boudicca was feeling tough and tired – an indisputable outcome from the night before. She took a moment to look at the pattern on Nonie's waterproof table cover, blue teapots overflowing with small blue and purple flowers. 'Nothing ... nothing at all,' she replied.

The officers nodded with professional smiles.

'Do you know something you're not telling me?' asked Boudicca, still looking at the table cover.

CI Jones's smile melted and his face grew serious.

The inspector's hand dived into his bag and pulled out a tablet, flipped it open, and swiped the screen. His hands were different to Prospero's, Boudicca thought. Prospero would call them "inside hands" – unused to outside work.

'There is something you might like to see,' he said, typing in a security code. The crest of the Thames Valley police appeared on the screen. On it a swan standing on a helmet holding a sword, supported by a red stag and ox chained beside a sign reading "Sit pax In Vale Tamesis". Boudicca's thoughts turned quickly to the Ullaunites coat of arms, the rising salmon surrounded by stars and its own Latin inscription "Somnia Sine Metu".

'We have traced your mother's last known sighting to the Bodleian library, in Oxford' CI Jones began. 'We have the CCTV footage, it may jog your memory.'

'Would you like us to show it to you Boudicca?' asked Officer Hickey.

'Of course.' Boudicca's voice was impatient.

CI Jones moved the tablet, sliding it in front of her. The footage was grainy, black and white, showing rows of shelving filled with books. From the side, Boudicca's mother appeared, walking into frame. She had a bag slung over her shoulder and opened it, removed something from it. She then moved out of sight, hidden by a row of shelves. The footage stopped. A silence hung over the group.

'That's it?' announced Prospero. 'That's all you have?'

'Yes,' said CI Jones, almost apologetically, 'we're still awaiting footage from other sources.'

Prospero was becoming agitated. 'You came all the way from Oxford … with that!'

Nonie gave him a look to calm or vacate the kitchen. Muttering to himself, he left. Officer Hickey took the lead.

'We are wondering if it jogs your memory. Maybe your mother said something. Where she was going or who she was going to meet in the Library?' she suggested.

Boudicca was calm. 'Officer Hickey, my mother works in the Medieval Linguistics Department, in Oxford. She goes to that library every day. It is her place of work. The only thing it jogs in my memory is that she used that library every day.'

Garda Hickey found Boudicca's calmness unusual for a child in her position, yet she remained professional.

'Have you footage of her leaving the library?' asked Boudicca.

'No, not yet,' CI Jones replied, touching the tips of his fingers together.

Boudicca moved to the computer. 'May I?'

C I Jones nodded.

Reviewing the footage again, Boudicca skipped repeatedly back and forth to the bit where her mum removed something from her bag. She couldn't see it in enough detail. But it looked familiar, like one of the books from the Omnium Gatherum the previous night. 'So, she may have disappeared in the library,' said Boudicca.

Garda Hickey tut-tutted and took this to be impertinence on the girl's behalf.

CI Jones politely followed the line of enquiry. 'That is a possibility, but not a likely one. We have searched the library and she's not there.'

'I didn't say she was hiding there,' said Boudicca, 'I said "disappeared" there.'

'This must be very hard for you,' said Officer Hickey, her mouth turned down, bottom lip proud in practiced empathy, but Boudicca saw it as matronising.

Boudicca looked into her eyes. 'Define hard?'

Garda Hickey furrowed her brow, straightened her mouth and stiffened her jaw.

'If you think of anything else, however small, make sure your let us know,' said C I Jones.

'I will,' said Boudicca.

Pleasant smiles were exchanged and Nonie led the officers out of the house.

Boudicca returned to her bedroom. She sat at her desk, glancing at her phone, still expecting a message from her mother. She trawled through her gallery of photos of them together, replaying videos of memorable days out with her mother: the London Eye, Covent Garden, Portobello Road, Electric Avenue, Kew Gardens. The videos made her sad. Boudicca felt as if her bones were hollow and her blood cold. She lay on her bed and cried without inhibition, deeper than she had ever cried before, fearing the videos would replace memories, or that the memories would vanish with time.

Nonie entered and sat on the edge of the bed, placing her hand on Boudicca's back, who got up and instinctively hugged her grandmother.

'It's hard, Grandma' sobbed Boudicca, unaware of the snot and spit left on Nonie's blouse. The union between the pair was forged stronger in the embers of a glowing grief. Boudicca missed her mum and Nonie missed her daughter.

'Let's go for a walk,' said Nonie. 'It's a most beautiful day.'

The suggestion was greeted with sniffs and nods.

The sun was shining. Swallows skimmed low across the tops of the flowering meadows. The blooms danced in the light breeze, as did the bees, buzzing the chorus of the summer. In the sunlight, grandmother and granddaughter walked through fields, ignored by contented cows that chewed their cud and pondered nothing but that same contentment.

They reached the edge of Lake Leane. The sun glistened off the still water like it was tin foil. Climbing an outcropping of rock overlooking the lake, the pair sat and took in the beauty of the view.

'I used to come here with your mother when she was your age,' Nonie said.

Boudicca smiled at the thought of a younger Nonie.

'I wasn't a fan of the water,' said Nonie, sizing up the lake with squinting eyes. 'Your mum would say that it was a waste to be so close to water and not swim.'

'She was right,' confirmed Boudicca. 'I mean she is right.'

'She is. Your mother is rarely wrong,' replied Nonie. 'It is a terrible thing to lose someone so dear while so young, but things only remain lost until they are found. You have to remember that.' Nonie felt like she had said too much.

'I can swim in the swimming pool alright,' said Nonie, after a time.

'I know.'

'But not today!' Nonie smiled.

Boudicca looked at her grandmother with a puzzled expression. 'Eh?'

'I've seen pictures of you Boudicca. You can swim,' said Nonie.

'I'm ok.'

'Well then?'

'Well then what?'

'Let's have a swim,' Nonie said, excitedly.

'Ok. We can go back and get our swimming costumes.'

'No, no, no. I'm talking here, now!' There was a nervous lightness in Nonie's voice.

'Now? Are you mad?' Boudicca's eyes were bulging.

'Maybe,' said Nonie, she peered into the water's depths. 'I've always been too scared to jump off this rock. I don't know why, it's plenty deep, but I never could. Too afraid, you see.'

Boudicca smiled at her energetic rebellion against age.

'What say you?' asked Nonie, getting to her feet, kicking off her shoes.

'What are you doing?'

'I'm kicking off my shoes.'

'Why?'

'Because I don't want to get them wet when I jump off this rock into the water, with you, in ten seconds time,' said Nonie, scarcely believing her own words.

'With me?' Boudicca laughed.

'I'll jump if you will?' asked Nonie.

Boudicca smiled at the challenge.

'At any age, there are times when we are braver together than we are alone child,' Nonie said.

'You're on, ' replied Boudicca.

Boudicca kicked off her trainers, taking a moment to look at her little weakling foot with its crescent of toes. She felt the locket under her t-shirt. They took a step back, their hands clasped together and then ran as quick as they could. A quick glance between the pair and they squealed and jumped into the cold water below, plunging with a mighty splash. They laughed and screeched in hysterics, feeling the icy water on their skin. The cows in the fields raised their heads momentarily at the trills and then lowered them again.

Leaving the lake, the swimmers were summer warmed. They walked the fields together. The sun was shining and the swallows skimmed low across the tops of the flowering meadows. The blooms danced in the light breeze as did the bees, buzzing the chorus of the summer an octave lower now. As the grandmother and granddaughter walked, they were ignored by contented cows that chewed their cud, who pondered the pressure on their dugs and the release of that afternoon's milking.

The pair hugged Prospero spontaneously, as they returned to the cottage.

'Ye're drowned,' he said, in surprise.

'Tis only water,' replied Nonie. 'How's Paddy's mare?'

'Still in the shakes but time will tell,' replied a sombre Prospero. He looked at their wet hair.

'Were ye swimming in the lake?'

'Yes,' replied Boudicca, triumphantly.

'In yer clothes?'

'We didn't skinny dip. We wouldn't want to offend the neighbours or the tourists,' said Nonie, with a wink to Boudicca.

'March hares the two of ye.' Prospero returned to his office.

Dried and in her bedroom, Boudicca took out the book from the locket and lay on her bed. It was dry, unaffected by the water. To her amazement, the words on the pages were now legible under the magnifying glass, and some writing had changed to clear English, yet the handwriting still her mother's.

The paragraphs seemed to describe the lives of different animals and what they did, how they seemed to feel or think as they did things. The words felt right sitting in her mind and they had a known weight to them, as if familiar and off-by-heart. It reminded her of the Ullanites and how they worked with the animals of nature. She was certain that this was a message from her mother, and however scared she felt, or upset she was, it was a message that must be heeded.

'Things are only lost until they are found,' she thought, placing the book into the locket again. Boudicca picked up her prescription black boots from the floor. She took them to the kitchen where Nonie was drying her hair with a tea towel. 'Have you any grease Grandma?' asked Boudicca.

'Under the sink.'

Boudicca found the shoe grease, and began to cover her boots at the kitchen table, in silence.

When done, Boudicca limped to Nonie who had returned to the kitchen in a change of clothes. Boudicca gave her a hug. 'We're braver together,' she said, before making for her room.

Nonie's eyes welled as she watched her grandchild limp down the corridor, polished boots in hand.

Boudicca put her boots beside the bed, waiting for the evening to slip away off the edge of the earth and for the night to come. She now found herself amongst quiet moments, and her fear did roar.

# Chapter 7

The Book of Alkaid

*Chapter 88*
*Verse 106*

*On the wren's nest*

*A short flight toward the morning star, a young female has a fine nest in a thicket of blackberry. Tasty work, I knew her mother. She had many failures with nests before, but that wren learned. For through failure there is either death or mastery.*

*A cat caught her one night most recent, her heart stopped with the shock of being unfree. The very idea of it killed her. The same cat left her on a wall out of pure carelessness.*

Blood made a tiny rivulet down the side of Ashket Giorra's face. Her eyes were still closed. Her arms and legs swayed with every step that Olor took.

Approaching Mount Bolcawn, Olor made his way up the rock face, through clouds, unerring in his footing and reaching the south-facing outcrop with his prize limp under his arm. Locating a concealed section of rock, he easily moved it to one side to reveal a dark passageway. Head bowed, he entered the inner Chamber of Mustela, the grand cathedral of the Regnum in the province of Muan. His cohort of Robusti followers huddled at the entrance, not daring to take another step. Olor was not Robustus. He was a Grafter – a human taken from the earth and added to by the Regnum to suit its need. Once the norm, he was now a grotesque oddity that encouraged thought of times before. A time of origins. In this time, thoughts of origin were dangerous and not tolerated under the Regnum. Olor was a thing of difference. In the Regnum, difference was to be feared and summarily wiped from memory.

The passage opened up to a cavernous space, completely dark save for a torch lit on the wall, guarded by Decima, the Praetorian guard. She stood there hawkish, the height of an elephant. Her skin pale, muscles swelled her face. Her eyes bulging in relief sitting inside sunken sockets. She was dressed in a black habit, the cowl on her head. Olor saw the cat-o'-nine-tails whip that hung from her belt. Decima walked behind him, the ends of each strap on the whip swung and bumped on the side of her leg. As Olor entered, the long play of shadows danced from the torchlight, revealing the height of the chamber. He grabbed the torch from the wall and lowered it into a puddle on the floor, which immediately caught fire. The flames grew along channels on the walls, encircling the immense space in a moment – in the middle of which sat a dark pit.

Olor's arrival also signalled by the sound of tiny squeals from the darkness. Imperceptible at first, the squeals began to grow in volume. As they grew, Olor's apprehension grew with it. From the pit, a black hillock of rolling weasels emerged. The seething mass rose to the height of two men and remained bound in their profusion. Their ever-rising numbers pushed and gushed forth in perfect synchronous motion towards Olor. Then, as soon as it began, the massed body halted. The weasels began to peel back. Emerging from within their confusion was Mustela, sitting on his throne.

'Divide et Impera,' called Olor, with a bow.

'Divide et Impera,' came the whispered reply, from the mound.

'I have brought you an Ullaunite. A girl. Sister of Finn Giorra. May her oil bring power and glory to you and the Regnum.' Olor bowed again.

Mustela's skin was translucent white, grotesquely exaggerated by the full-length white smock that he wore. Mustela had an angular body that looked like it had been drained of blood and filled with milk. A ridge of hair grew on the edge of a baldpate, a border on his dome in a monastic style. His face was a collection of jutting angles, black lips concealed jaundiced teeth, fingers disproportionately long that exposed the pronounced outline of vein and bone. With a mouth that barely moved, but the sound of his breath filled the space, Mustela inhaled deeply, sensing the amount of Anam in the blood of the captured Ullaunite lying prostrate before him.

'You have failed,' he said.

The weasels squealed in delight as Olor's worst fears became realised.

'I grow weary of your failure.' Mustela sighed. 'This is not the Ursine.'

'Sire, it is an Ullaunite.'

'The Ullaunites are bedraggled and their end is soon to come. They are no longer my concern. The capturing of the Ursine, however, is. As such, this is a failure. I deem it a failure. If I deem it so, then it is so,' said Mustela, with barely a flicker of emotion. He let his verdict stand. 'Collect the Ullaunite!' he ordered.

A slew of weasels rolled forward to form a platform. Olor dutifully placed Ashket on top of this fleshy heaving dais. The rodents wrapped around her limbs, neck and face. They filled her pockets, feeling for her returners with their nimble claws and removing them. Ashket was ferried away on a river of pelts.

'You are a Grafter, the last amongst my forces. You are becoming …' Mustela thought a moment, 'too different. I worry for your safety. They plot your downfall, you know?'

Olor remained silent.

'We keep returning to this problem, do we not? Again and again. You are different Olor, smell different, sound different. You do not blend in. You cannot be hidden.' Mustela looked over Olor's shoulder at the gathered mob crowding the entrance. 'There is dissent in your mob. Ambition nibbles their nails. They all want what you have. All wish to be Lictor. All wish to kill you for it. To be different is one thing, but to be different amongst conformity, well that's … fatal.' Mustela allowed his last words to linger in the silence.

Olor could hear his own breathing, heightened and echoed by the chamber. Broken only by the collective howl from behind, Blacktooth raised his head and stood on his back legs.

Mustela baited the crowd further. 'We are greater numbers now and we can run them down. We no longer have need for your cleverness. And truthfully, I suspect you. I suspect your loyalty. I do. I do.'

With this verdict, Mustela had effectively signed Olor's death sentence. Any defence was pointless. He would now have to fend off attacks from those wishing to take over.

A taproot of weasels made its way from beneath Mustela's chair. It grew out sinuously and wrapping around Olor's legs, up past his knees, thighs and chest. Beads of sweat grew on his brow and his breathing turned to a laboured wheeze.

'Take your oil, Lictor,' barked Mustela.

A weasel grabbed a glass vial of bright yellow liquid from Mustela's open hand. It scampered toward Olor, who thought it to be a reprieve, a salutary lesson. But the weasel ran past him.

'Blacktooth,' Mustela called, 'step forward.'

Blacktooth returned to knuckle and foot, obsequiously grovelling forward, his cheek and chin rubbing along the dusted floor, smearing himself in the damp dirt.

The weasel climbed Blacktooth's hand, fearlessly to his gapping mouth, where it dropped the vial on his tongue.

Mustela looked at the petrified Blacktooth. 'You see Olor, this is the advantage of conformity. Look at him – half crazed with fear, created ill and by my command, instructed to be well. Drink your oil Lictor. Feel its power,' said a triumphant Mustela.

Blacktooth took the vial from his mouth, popped the cork and gulped it down in one, licking his lips at the intoxicating taste. His body shook. Steam rose from his skin like that of a just galloped mare. The muscles on his body quivered, growing bigger and more powerful with each moment. Blacktooth felt energised, instantly more alert and intelligent, roaring at his metamorphosis.

'Divide et Impera,' he thundered, his voice no longer in minion squeal.

None of the mob looked to Olor anymore, only to Blacktooth. Silently Mustela walked to him along a pelt path. The weasels continued to squeeze the air out of Olor's lungs, pressing on veins, bearing their fangs and awaiting orders.

Mustela continued with a calmer voice. 'You fail me because you are different. Not your fault. But I am nothing if not merciful. I first thought that I should kill you now and let whatever little cunning you have die with you.' He continued, smiling with yellow teeth, 'and then I thought. There's something else that you can do for the Regnum. Another service to the state.' Mustela banished his sneer with black lips. 'I thought, for you to be sacrificed to the new Lictor, would fortify the bond between him and his new mob. Esprit de corps, et cetera.'

Olor knew his time was up.

'Blacktooth,' called Mustela.

Blacktooth moved forward, his black fang proportionately bigger in his mouth.

'It is time for you to take control of your mob,' ordered Mustela. 'The Lictor is dead, long live the Lictor.'

The weasels released their grip on Olor, called to heel by their master.

Blacktooth stood above the weakened victim, revelling in his new size, strength and keenness of mind. He picked up Olor by the neck and tossed him against the wall. The mob cheered on their new leader as he pummelled Olor with a savage flurry of blows. Olor was picked up and then slammed to the ground. The mob sensed a kill was near. Olor felt he had one chance of escape, if that. It would mean leaving the chamber by the way he had entered.

More of Blacktooth's blows rained down, throwing him around like a doll. After one such blow, Olor landed near the wall of the cavern, next to the puddle of burning oil. This was his chance. He waited a moment, taking what he thought might be his last breath as Blacktooth and his cohort crowded in on him – saliva dripping from their enamel. Olor then buried his hand in the puddle of burning oil and kept it there without registering the pain on his skin. He waited for the mob to draw close. As they did, he scooped up the burning oil and threw it at them. The diversionary fireball bought him a few seconds as he ran toward the opening – punching, kicking and biting everything and anything that got in his way.

Reaching the moonlight, he knew each stride would take him away from execution but directly to the cliff edge. Olor jumped off the cliff face, into the abyss.

The mob followed to the edge and howled in annoyance at the loss of the kill. A livid Blacktooth screamed impetuously, like a murderous child who had mislaid a plaything. It was the last thing Olor heard as he fell into thick clouds, his arm on fire and toward certain death.

# Chapter 8

The Book of Dubhe

*Chapter 532*
*Verse 991*

*On a March Hare entering the fray*

*In the first moon, the blood heats and I know it's coming and I smell the air and there is the heart's endeavour on it, and we all smell it. I look for opponents and I would be disappointed and disrespected if they did not look for me,*

*Oh when you catch them flush, their mettle is tested. Their eyes tell everything their paws can't, the tufts of hair softly returning to earth.*

*When my mettle breaks, for it will, I will fall away, and my end will follow and I will drown in a ditch somewhere unknown or be surprised by a stupid young dog, ignorant of my once magisterial name.*

Finn was motionless on the side of his bed. His eyes scanned the items in the room. A dried posey his sister had picked moons ago, a hair tie, pieces of paper with her handwriting. He turned his head away not wishing to see them as momentuous and thus magnify his loss.

'She is not gone. She is not gone,' Finn whispered, to himself. He calmly rejoined the others at the fire. Their chatter dampened down as soon as he appeared. None wished to speak of Ashket in his presence. 'Where is Boudicca?' he asked.

'Returned home,' said Gannymeade, matter-of-factly.

Though disappointed by the news, it seemed to urge him on. 'We must go to Mount Bolcawn, then,' he exhorted.

Gannymeade's expression didn't change. The eyes of the group were on her now. 'Finn ….'

Finn gave a low cough, as he attempted to bridle emotions that were frothing at the bit.

Gannymeade took the opportunity to speak. 'I cannot know how you feel right now, Finn, but we should take a moment.'

'I don't have the luxury of a moment,' he snapped, 'we either survive or we die, these are the options. It is stark and clear, now. It is nature.'

Gannymeade straightened, thinking it wiser to listen than interrupt.

'The Regnum grow stronger, more numerous and more deadly by the day. We have no option. If we keep going this way, it will be death by a thousand cuts. The inevitable will happen.' Finn's eyes were ablaze.

'We can't. Not right now,' replied Gannymeade. 'My strategy is to keep us alive for as long as we can.'

'I understand. We wouldn't be here without you. None would be alive without your stratagem and power of protection. But she is my sister, Gannymeade. Do you understand?'

Gannymeade spoke, 'Your hurt is deep, Finn, but we must stay together. We cannot take them on like this. A full engagement with their numbers would overwhelm us, and that definitely would be the end. If we fight like that, we are gone and he has won.'

Finn cleared his throat again. 'I just want her safe. That's all. I promised her that I would protect her – and I have failed. I cannot die failing that duty.'

The fire seemed to react to Finn's energy, and dimmed. Gannymeade took her pipe from her waistcoat pocket, tapered it and puffed it back to full strength.

'We cannot attack them front on. Let us think a moment and see if there is another way,' she mused.

Finn stared at and poked the fire. It flickered into life. As did Finn, when a thought suddenly struck. 'I know what you wait for,' said Finn, looking straight at Gannymeade.

Gannymeade puffed in silence.

'You're waiting for The Ursine to restore the Child of Bears. You believe in the myth. This is not a story with a happy ending,

Gannymeade,' said Finn.

Gannymeade nodded calmly and responded, 'We will strike when the time is right. We have our magic and our skills, something we must rely on. Ashket has been taken, like many before. But the Ullaunite tribe is only us now. We are it. Once gone, there is nothing – nothing – to stop him and his evil growing boundless. The next step could be our last.'

'Ashket's magic was no defence,' Finn said, in a voice low.

'The next step could be our last,' Gannymeade repeated.

Finn took a moment.

No one spoke.

'I agree,' he replied.

Finn rose from his seat and made to leave, waiting a moment at the door. 'Gannymeade, you are the matriarch, my leader. I wish no other to lead us. I will follow you to the end. Little seed was collected before the attack, let me collect oak and alder seed, as originally planned.'

Gannymeade looked to him, suspicious of his change of heart but realized he was right. Tycho nodded.

'Take Constantina and Tarquin with you,' Gannymeade replied after a time.

Finn left with a bow.

◆          ✝          ◆

Ashket weakly opened her eyes and saw the dusted floor pass beneath her. She was held by two muscular Robusti, separated from her returners and thus weak of her life force.

The hallway led to a door, which opened to a chamber filled with the sound of pistons and mechanics. As they entered, blue and yellow lights flickered on in the distance, illuminating rows of glass tanks on stands, in all directions, filling the cavernous space.

Ashket blinked, barely taking in the monstrous picture that lay before her, as she passed a line of circular glass tanks on either side of the walkway, each standing three meters high. She spied the Robusti looking at their contorted reflections on the curve of the tanks.

Lights appeared on the tanks to one side. She was shocked to see an Ullanite child, suspended in a clear blue liquid. This was followed by another tank containing an old man, stripped to his under garments. His eyes were covered with bandages. His head tilted, a needle puncturing the skin above his heart, another needle coming out of his forehead. Both attached to the roof of the tank. The old man's arms and legs hung, the nerves in his muscles twitched sporadically. Ashket saw his index finger moved intermittently, pulsing the rhythm of some lost memory.

Ashket couldn't tell how long the space was, but there were rows and rows of these tanks as far as her eyes could see. All containing suspended and tubed Ullaunites, bathed and embalmed in their Anam draining stasis. Above them, Robusti gathered and looked down from gangways. She saw a dark tank light up. This, too, filled with a blue liquid, two pipes with pins floating in it, like the roots of a water lily. Ashket was so overcome by weakness and despair that she passed out again.

Moments later, she was stripped of all but her armlets and in undergarments, bandaged, piped and suspended in the tank. The slow methodical sound of a pump whizzed and as she calmly slept, Ashket's extraction had begun.

◆　　✦　　◆

The Fia gathered and brought Finn, Tarquin, and Constantina deep into the forest where the oak and alder seed lay in abundance. They set about their work, opening their pouches and collecting the seed.

Constantina leant back, looking up, feeling the moonlight on her face. After some clicking, she could see dew droplets collecting on new webs, a dampness in the air that made it crisp yet heavy. The oak leaves hung hefty on branches; fern fronds bowed beneath their dew-soaked weight. The ground under foot was wet. This was a place where the sensile oak and alder grew in nuptial bliss, both plants helping each other grow.

There was the sound of a branch snapping in the darkness.

'What was that?' whispered Finn.

'Hold,' said Constantina, 'don't move.' She clicked, facing the murky beyond. The Ullaunites felt their returners.

'What can you see?' Finn asked.

Constantina continued clicking, scanning the landscape. Something fluttered from a bush. To their relief, it was just a bird, barely visible.

'A warbler,' Tarquin called, 'just a warbler.'

They returned to their picking. All except Constantina, who as of yet, was unconvinced. She clicked – slowly at first and then with increasing speed. Not looking beyond the trees but at them, through them. Constantina held her hand out, a sign that did not go unnoticed by the others. Their wariness returned. No one moved.

'Can you see it?' asked Constantina. 'The trees? They are ...'

'What?' asked Tarquin.

'... alive,' she finished.

'We know that,' replied Tarquin, wincing at the obvious nature of the comment.

'No, you don't understand – they are breathing,' replied Constantina.

Scanning the darkness, she called at the top of her voice, 'ROBUSTI!'

Instantly the tree bark fell away, revealing hundreds of Robusti, sitting on each other's shoulders in hiding. They pounced down in their multitudes. The Ullaunites immediately adopted a defensive formation. Blacktooth stood on a rock beyond, howling orders and signals. His twisted muscular torso advertised gargantuan strength and recent development.

'Blacktooth!' shouted Tarquin.

'He has grown,' said Finn.

'A new lictor. Olor must be dead,' said Tarquin.

Blacktooth looked on in his immensity. His eyes were quicker too.

'We must split, or we will all be trapped,' said Finn, seeing a complete encirclement.

'Agreed,' said Constantina, clicking furiously.

Tarquin and Constantina ran and slashed their way west, Finn did the same to the east. Greatly outnumbered, the Ullaunites fought with vigour. Their skill with their returners began cutting swathes through the opposing forces. Fighting with venomous power, the Ullaunites kicked, punched and ripped with awesome precision. Robusti fell by the score but yet they had confidence in their numbers. Finn deliberately isolated himself. By coaxing the attention of Blacktooth, and drawing numbers away from the others, Finn could tempt them in the chance of success – and Anam oil.

'Constantina!' Finn called, taking the pouch from his shoulder containing oak and alder seed. He threw it to her.

As she caught it, she spin-kicked a Robusti, with her heel. She knew what Finn was about to do. 'No, Finn. You will be hunted down!'

'I cannot fail her.' Finn turned to Blacktooth, and called across to him. 'Blacktooth, follow me and I will fight you all.'

'Lead the way little rabbit,' replied Blacktooth.

'I am a hare – join me in a dance.' Finn ran into the black shadows.

In his excitement, Tarquin threw his returner too hard, impaling it – and a Robustus – on a tree. Other Robusti leapt on it to make sure it did not return to Tarquin's hand. He stood there weaponless and feeling immediately weakened without it. Seeing this, others directed their assault in earnest, and from different sides. Tarquin's parrying skills were beginning to wane as Robusti punches and kicks found their mark. Constantina was now defending both of them. The tide was turning, they could not keep this pace going. The Robusti knew it too.

'Retrieve your returner, Tarquin,' she shouted.

'I cannot. They have swarmed it,' shouted Tarquin, barely deflecting another punch. They were in serious trouble.

Just then, Tarquin saw the shadow of a figure leap through the air from the high rocks behind. As it emerged into the moonlight and landed, Tarquin recognised the Fia with the white stripe. He also recognised the rider on its back: Boudicca Moriarty.

In her leather livery, Boudicca took out her returners and began to fight. Her Fia used its antlers to attack the Robusti that had gathered around Tarquin's returner, and sent them flying. Tarquin called to his now freed returner again. As the sword spun and returned, so did his confidence and power. The Robusti scattered and joined Finn's chasing pack. Suddenly, the Ullaunites were alone.

'Good to see you, Boudicca,' said Tarquin. 'Your timing is impeccable.'

'You came back?' asked Constantina, her tone a mixture of surprise and delight.

Boudicca offered a hand up to Constantina and Tarquin. They both mounted the Fia.

'What about Finn?' she asked.

'He is gone,' said Constantina.

Boudicca clicked to the Fia, who turned and then bolted back through the pathless fern groves.

# Chapter 9

The Book of Mizar

Chapter 83

Verse 4196

*An artic tern watches the tide*

*Sand banks appear on the coast of the dying star, we are in the tenth moon and the Boreals blow wild and it is as much as we can do to master them. The small cod are rising and the sandy floor drives them up. We will watch them be foolish on the banks, waiting to dive, swoop and feast.*

*The sea is my land. I fear nothing here.*

*Foxes and owls, they fear the sea.*

*I do not fear the sea.*

Now the calm.

The only things he could hear were his breathing and the pulse of his barely beating heart. His skin was in goose bumps, lips trembling. Finn stopped, and stillness poured over him. He could hear the buzzing of bees from miles away, the muffled chirping of linnet chicks, using egg teeth to crack through their shells. He could hear the last breath and prayer of an old badger vacating his sett, to die safely away from his kin, happy with his years and fights. All these sounds comingled in Finn's ears, pooling there in a glorious aria.

He held his returner a little less tightly. He was calm, knowing he had drawn away the attention of the Robusti mob from the others, allowing them to escape. A great fight had taken place and he knew the level of his violence reached was high, even by his own preternatural standards. It was at times like these that an Ullaunite reached the summit of their bloody euphoria. He was the most senior of the fighting Ullaunites. Today again was another reminder to the Regnum, that few could match an Ullaunite's skills even with overwhelming numbers.

Slowly he breathed his way back to normality and away from the realm of the hare. Around him lay thousands of Robusti bodies in deathly repose. His Ullaunite leathers were drenched in sweat and blood, drops of both falling from his knuckles. Beneath him was Blacktooth – breathless, broken and on his knees. The edge of Finn's returner squarely at his neck.

'Do it!' said Blacktooth, almost praying for a quick release from the shame of returning to Mustela vanquished, being released of his lictorship, and thrown to the mob.

Finn leaned into Blacktooth. 'You knew where we were. Who told you?'

Blacktooth said nothing.

'Who told you where we were?'

Silence.

'Let me speak a language you understand.' Finn sliced off the top of Blacktooth's nose.

The beast roared as blood gushed out and over his mouth.

'Who told you where we were?'

'Mustela,' quivered Blacktooth.

'How did he know?'

'I don't know.'

Finn sensed he was telling the truth. To Blacktooth's surprise, Finn stepped back, unbuckled his sheath and laid his weaponry on the ground in front of him.

'You should be dead, but I will not kill you today,' said Finn, unarmed.

Blacktooth remained on his knees, eyes wide, nose still bleeding profusely.

'Ask me why?' said Finn.

'Why?' said Blacktooth, cautiously.

'I look at your growing numbers as a child considers the sea, and I am overwhelmed. I cannot comprehend its end or its beginning. I cannot fight it anymore. I wish an extraction and for it to be as painless as possible,' said Finn, 'that is why.'

Blacktooth scrunched his face in confusion.

'You may return with me as your reward,'said Finn.

The Ullaunite scanned the ground. Beneath a lifeless body, he saw a sizeable rock sitting snug in the earth. Bending over he loosened it. Blacktooth rose from his hands and curiously looked on.

'To capture an Ullaunite, as senior as me – with as much Anam oil as me – and to present that Ullaunite to Mustela after your first hunt, would be quite the catch, would it not? Think of the oil. Why your cups would overflow,' said Finn, holding the rock.

The thought kept Blacktooth focused.

'Present me to Mustela, and let the rewards be yours,' Finn solemnly ordered.

He tossed the rock high, looking at it soar. Above its path, an Artic tern glided by, rapt in the power of the winds above. Finn returned his gaze to Blacktooth, his face at peace. 'There are times when you know the fight is lost and that the tipping point has passed. The Regnum cannot be defeated and nature will be brought to heel. Your power will triumph and the Ullauns will be yours. I am done with this fight and want to be near my sister when it ends.'

Finn bent forward. Blacktooth watched in disbelief as he deliberately let the falling rock crack into his skull, knocking him unconscious. He fell to the forest floor motionless. Blacktooth moved forward furtively. The most senior Ullaunite warrior lay prone before him, unconscious and unarmed. Blacktooth slipped the returners over his shoulder and saw a sizeable gash on the back of his head, oil and blood seeping from the wound. The sight excited him. He slowly placed his claw on the wound, dabbing the seeping oil and touching it to his mouth. The taste made him dizzy and unsteady on his feet. This Ullaunite was full of oil for sure!

Bending on one knee and with great restraint, Blacktooth grabbed Finn by the waistcoat and held him up to survey his small size. He glanced quickly around the forest, scanning the dead, satisfied that no life could be discerned in any eye. This Ullaunite had done a thorough job. Blacktooth leaped forward with Finn over his shoulder – like a shepherd carrying a lamb – and returned to Mount Bolcawn to claim his prize.

# Chapter 10

The Book of Alioth

*Chapter 9837*

*Verse 280*

*On brown trout after heavy rains*

*Darkness everywhere. All are blind. We are in the seventh moon, and the star has not been seen for some time and the grey covers all. On these times, we go low, we go to the bottom. Below rainwater we are safe and the pike is blind also.*

The remaining Ullaunites were grief stricken. Word had filtered through that their most senior comrade had been captured and would soon be extracted by the Regnum, with his Anam oil strengthening the enemy even further. Sitting around the fire in Cumann Rock, silence turned to suspicion.

'How did they know where the group was?' Ithaca's brow furrowed in disbelief.

'We don't know,' Tycho grumbled, under wisps of pipe smoke.

'Robusti are known for their numbers, but not their intelligence,' continued Ithaca.

'Olor is,' said Niamh.

'It wasn't Olor,' said Constantina, 'it was Blacktooth.'

'Finn led them there,' said Alba.

An uneasy feeling settled and the faces turned to Alba.

'What are you saying?' said Tarquin, bristling.

Alba, took her pipe from her mouth and used it to emphasise her point. 'I'm saying he is the one who led you to the seed.'

'So?' pressed Tarquin, his head turned slightly in disblief.

'My point has been made,' Alba rebuffed, her teeth clenching on her pipe.

'More clearly then,' Tarquin's jaw jutting with annoyance.

'The group was ambushed by a prepared group – an enemy in waiting.'

'Are you are saying Finn lead us into an ambush?' Tarquin glowered beneath his eyebrows.

'Whether knowing it or not, he did.'

Tarquin's face widened. 'I can't believe you'd say that!'

'It's a fact,' replied Alba.

'Why would he do that? He is the most decorated of us all and protected more seed gatherings than you or I put together.' Tarquin was clearly incensed.

'He is also grieving,' Alba puffed, calmly. 'His mind is clouded with grief for his sister. He has wanted to engage them since she was taken.'

The bickering and chatter grew. Others were drawn in.

Boudicca kept her head down and remained silent. She noticed Gannymeade take a little capsule from her waistcoat pocket and throw into the fire. Seconds later, a mighty ball of flame exploded and leapt from the fire, breaking everyone's concentration. Alba and Tarquin turned and hung their heads.

Gannymeade stood there, her face set hard. 'You are right, Alba, but in the same breath you are wrong,' said Gannymeade, in a re-assured voice. 'Finn is not the only one who knows the details of the collections. He receives that information from someone else.'

All eyes searched in suspicion.

'Who?' asked Constantina.

'Me,' replied Gannymeade.

No one had suspected the Matriarch – not for a second. The group was hushed, as if fearing what Gannymeade would reveal next.

'I am the source. I receive the information from the Bradán in a dream. So you see, I could also be the one who betrayed the position to the Regnum – and not Finn.'

'It can't be you,' said Tarquin.

'Why not me? Mustela and the Regnum are so powerful now that everyone is prey.'

'But it's you, Gannymeade,' said Tarquin, his face slack in disbelief.

'That means nothing. In defending the Ullauns, many heads have been turned by the promise of power. You only have to think of the Night of Harrows,' said Gannymeade. 'Alba is thinking clearly. And that is what we need right now, we must consider all, be aware of all.' Gannymeade puffed and took a moment. 'Since Ashket was taken, I've been sleeping poorly. Broken, in fits and starts. I thought it was the worry of losing her, but now I am not so sure. The day before Ashket's abduction, I dreamed the manner in which she would go. I was there. I saw it all – Olor's trap. At first I did not believe it, so I set it aside as the wanderings of my million moon mind.'

Gannymeade paused. She looked at her fingers and then to all the disbelieving faces. The only exceptions were Tycho who looked down and Old Joe who looked away. 'When you get older, you begin to doubt yourself.' She cleared her throat. 'I had two more dreams. One dream happened tonight, where Finn was taken – chapter and verse as I had seen it. That is why I didn't want him to go.'

'You knew he would be taken?' asked Constantina. 'You still let us go.'

'Yes,' said Gannymeade, 'because I knew Boudicca would return.' She gave Boudicca a half-hearted smile.

'You said two more dreams. What of the other?' pressed Niamh.

Gannymeade stopped a moment. 'It was a dream of the Ullauns. No trees, no seed. Shrill winds, smoke and fire, all life devastated. The stars could not be seen for some time and the grey pall covered all. I believe it to be a vision of the end.'

'But you were the only one who saw these dreams?' asked Alba, looking for a sign of hope.

Gannymeade shook her head. 'I felt a darkness there with me in my dream, I cannot account for it. It was a presence familiar to me, and it saw everything I saw.'

'One of us?' asked Niamh.

Gannymeade did not reply, but only looked deeper into the fire. 'I am sorry. I have placed us in danger. The fate of both Ashket and Finn Giorra lie heavy on my mind and heart. I fear I may have led them to their end.'

Tycho put an arm of comfort around her. Gannymeade's eyes welled, her tears glinting in the firelight.

'I have sworn to protect all Ullaunites, Tycho. I am the Matriarch of the clan. I could not stop him. I have failed.' She quickly rose and retired to her quarters.

'It has been a long day,' said Tycho, wishing to comfort Gannymeade in her grief.

'We will meet again after a rest. Boudicca, you stay in Ashket's room.'

The group dispersed. The prevailing sense among them was that the bond of the last Ullaunites was broken. A deep trust was ruptured, their seam ripped asunder. Without a strong centre, like Gannymeade and her gravity, all would be lost to the edges. Old Joe was last to leave the fire.

Tarquin called him from the hallway, 'Dad? Dad?'

Old Joe looked up and threw the remainder of his tea on the flames and joined his son.

# Chapter 11

The Book of Megrez

*Chapter 891*
*Verse 29*

*A fox breaking*

*There is nothing purer than my run, I am so beautiful that I am consumed by the landscapes that secret me. I am the sublime. I am the celeste in stinking pelt. The stars made me. And when I break cover, I am in the swell of fear and joy and being chased is what I crave. It is then I am alive. It is then I am closest to death.*

Olor ran as fast as he could, fright and flight in every bound. He was still pursued by a mob. He had a giddiness in his chest, that mingled well with fear, at the very thought of avoiding his last breath. He made his way through gigantic fern fronds that seemed to open before him and close behind. He held his arm that was blistered and red. He appealed to a sanctuary of the shadows, before the smell of his blood would reveal him to the pack. In the near distance he could hear the sound of their barks and whistles. It was designed to unsettle him and drive him to the point he would break cover and be spotted.

The last thing he remembered from Mount Bolcawn was looking to the rock face as he fell through diaphanous clouds, arm aflame. He came to, when he hit the water below and could not believe his luck to have landed directly into a pool beneath a crack in the harsh rock, no one knew had existed. The crack was just wide enough to take the width of his diving body and deep enough to dissipate the energy of his landing. Slowly pulling himself up from between the rocks, he considered the opening and estimated that landing a millimetre on either side would have killed him outright.

A group of Robusti bolted past, turning their noses to the skies. They could smell his scent, yet were unable to see him. Olor held his breath and slipped behind a rock and instinctively closed his eyes, knowing they could hear his heart if they calmed themselves. But this group was too excited and enthused by the chase, blindly following the grunts of those in front. As they moved, Olor exhaled silently, controlling his breath as best he could.

Olor opened his eyes and found himself away from the woods of the Ullauns. Now standing in a mist-laden bog, where nothing of any beauty grew. In the distance, he saw a little hut, ruinous yet proud, on the land, defying the tyrannical bog on which it was built. Brown wet peat as far as the eye could see, no vegetation only harshness and acidity. An owl hooted in the mists beyond. Olor felt a coldness tighten his skin. He was staring at the hut. Rusted sedge and bulrush skirted its boundaries. He was in a different place now. The sounds of the chase were distant in his ears.

Without warning, he heard a deep breathing and the sound of lips being licked. It was coming from right behind him. He assumed he had been found and was almost relieved that the chase was over. Turning around he saw before him a creature, the height of three Robusti and the girth of seven. It was covered in a sleek black fur, a broad muzzled snout, like a bear, with great ram horns on its head. Massive sabre teeth projecting from each side of the mouth and eyes that blazed like flames in a dark storm. By Olor's reckoning, it was bigger than a Praetorian, which, until then, the biggest being he had ever seen. Immediately Olor sensed it to be an ancient thing.

The animal sniffed deeply. As it moved toward his face, Olor found little consolation in the warmth of its breath, which came with an overpowering smell of rotting flesh from massive canines. The creature's head alone was as big as his upper body, its nose as wide as two fists side by side. Olor looked at its great claws, waiting for one of them to end it all. There was a serenity in the moment that surprised the Grafter – no fear, no bravery, just a ceding control to the nature of the beast. Olor held the creature's look and saw the yellow eyes bubbling like lava.

'These were the eyes of a bright abyss,' he thought, 'and here is my end.'

The creature's mouth moved a little with a slopping sound as if cleaning its teeth with its tongue.

'Olor,' it spoke.

Olor swallowed whatever spit was left in his mouth. The creature could speak. Its voice was imbued with a tone that was Precambrian deep.

'How does it feel to be the enemy of the Regnum?' whispered the creature.

Olor nodded in stupefaction. 'Who are you?' he croaked, his mouth bone-dry.

'I am Pejanen Tyger.'

'What are you?' Olor probed.

'I am from a time before time and times itself,' replied the creature, moving beyond Olor. 'Now follow me.'

Pejenan Tyger said nothing as he walked toward the ruin, black puddles gathered in his paw prints. The wind was blowing on them now, mist rolling with it. On closer inspection of the hut, Olor could see the thatched roof in tatters, holes that coldly welcomed the weather. Some walls had crumbled, but what remained provided shelter from the wind. The mist drenched all it caressed.

'Why have you brought me here?' Olor asked, as he looked around.

Pejanen Tyger ignored him. Instead the beast sauntered forward, its rump a waddling mass of muscles beneath a deep black coat.

Olor tried again. 'Where are you from?'

No reply.

'Are you even from the Ullauns?'

'My kind roamed this land once in our multitudes,' said Pejanen, motionless now, 'well before the Regnum. You have no memory of this. Nobody does. Only we remember.'

The creature squeezed through the hut's broken doorway. Olor followed. They were shaded from the seeking wind that buffeted the corners outside.

'You have no memory, Olor,' said Pejanen, turning to give him his full attention.

'Of course I have memory,' Olor said.

'What is your first memory, then?'

Olor paused. 'It's serving the Regnum.'

'And before that?'

It was then Olor realised he could not remember anything. His memory – like his life – started with the Regnum.

Pejanen made for a far-off wall covered in old roots and he sniffed it. His attention then moved to a particular spot on the floor. Olor watched Pejanen claw at the dirt, moving the caked peat, revealing a buried shape, smooth and circular, a wooden post sawn off at the butt.

'You have no memory of this place?' Penjanen asked.

Olor shook his head.

'A good job was done on you then.'

Pejanen encouraged him forward. He invited Olor to stretch out his hand, lightly touching the butt in the ground with his claw. Olor slowly took the cue and put his hand on the stump and as he did so, an instant torrent of images came flooding back: a jumble of hellish screams, pleading, bloodletting, exposed bone, whipping with a cat-o'-nine-tails, knots, hooks, and blades. He heard the sounds of slicing and a frightful moaning. Shocked by this, he pulled his hand away, but it was too late. The seal on his memory had been broken. Nausea replaced shock as he squinted his eyes.

'Why have you brought me here?'

'To show you the work of your beloved Regnum.'

'All I see is a wooden stump in the floor.'

'You don't know what it is, do you?'

'No.'

'Yes, you do,' said Pajenan.

'I do not.'

The beast tapped his claw on the ground again. 'It is a flogging post. Mustela brought you here and broke you here. Took your memory and your Anam oil here, remade you here. Welcome to the first extraction house of the Regnum. The birthplace of the first Grafters.'

Olor's head dropped. In his mind the sounds returned. A chorus of gasps and gulps to the rhythm of the lash. Olor's face was drained of any emotion. He looked into Pejanen's eyes seeking answers.

'You are a Grafter, Olor, but you were not human to start with.'

'To be a Grafter you must have been human once. What was I, if not human?'

'Ullaunite. Something you still are.'

Olor exploded in a loud guffaw, then into uncontrollable laughter. 'Ullaunite!' He could barely get the word out.

'Yes, Ullaunite,' growled Pejanen. 'You know you are different. You don't look like them, don't think the same way.'

'That I know, but there are many glorious creations in the Regnum,' said Olor. 'I was once human and then as Mustela, in his glorious wisdom, he divided and conquered my nature and made me into a Grafter, to serve his will and that of the Regnum – Divide et Impera.'

Olor gave a respectful nod of his head.

'He called you Grafter, because you were one of the first to be extracted,' growled Pejanen. 'If he told you or anyone else that you were Ullaunite, well, you wouldn't have survived. For many moons you have chased the Anam oil in Ullaunites but once upon a time, you made your own.'

Olor was unmoved. 'I don't believe you. Lies, all lies. I was the first. Mustela engineered me.'

'It is a hard thing to come to terms with,' said Pejanen, trying to restore calm. 'But you are Ullaunite. You are not human. If you were human, you would have died, all those moons ago.'

Olor looked to the markings on the wall and then to the beast. 'If I am what you say I am, how have I survived? I have no returners. Are they not the mark of the Ullaunite – those blasted things.'

'Your Ullaunite cunning, made sure it survived. It's in your nature.'

Olor laughed out loud.

'A desperate logic, Tyger. Now I know you're lying.'

'You were a boy of four and three quarters. In the happiness of your first age, at one with nature, bound to it and nothing else. But you were stolen from your mother's bosom.'

'Lies.'

'Get a young Ullaunite child, reduce them to emptiness with purgation, create a vacuum and fill that vacuum with duty. Applying balm, as you drain him of his oil. It was what he needed for his plans to rule.'

Olor looked away as Pejanen persisted.

'When Mustela began his Regnum, he needed auxiliaries to wage his war against the Ancient Ullaunites. He convinced some of his fellow Ullaunites to join him, those who disagreed, paid the price.'

'That is your version of the Night of Harrows I suspect,' said Olor, 'a rebellion – as viewed by the vanquished.'

'Many returners flew that night,' recalled Pejanen. 'Mustela started a war, that persists today.'

'Not for long, the war will soon end,' said Olor, casting a furtive glance over his shoulder at the hut's interior.

•    +    •

Pejanen turned and left the hut. Outside he sat beside the stump of a bog oak, broken and rotten, its days of blossom and bud spent, the mist gathered in droplets on his fur.

Sometime later, and amongst the silence of the wind, Olor coughed to let him know he was there. Pejanen did not raise his head, his roaring yellow eyes instead focused on a peat puddle. Offing thunder rolled.

'How do you claim to know things that I don't even know myself?' began Olor.

'I know because I came to you when you were here. You pleaded to me to save you – but I could not.' Pejanen growled to clear his throat. Pejanen relived the memory himself.

'Another falsehood!' Olor felt a wave of nausea hit. His eyes could not focus. The mist confused and disorientated him. His hands trembled, tectonic shifts rumbling in the plates of his skull, gut and heart. 'You have to say something that only I know,' said Olor, 'otherwise you cannot be trusted.'

Both looked into the mist.

'How would I know something only you could know?' growled Pejanen.

'Find it, or I will know you are lying. And I will serve the Regnum to my last breath.'

Pejanen paused and looked out to the silent nothingness. 'The bracelet.'

Olor flinched and blinked.

'There was a bracelet on your wrist. It was solid gold with four swans on it, in relief, artistry in the work. You buried it. Here.'

Olor smiled, even though at that moment he had never felt more lost. He rolled on his heels, doing his best to stand steady.

'You are mistaken, Pejanen Tyger. Take me back to the pack that chase me.'

A drift of mist rolled in.

'One more thing,' said Pejanen.

In the blink of an eye, Olor found himself somewhere completely different.

◆     ✦     ◆

A magnificent lake stretched out before him. Around it, mountains standing sublime in ancient repose. Along their tops, he could see old winding paths. Gorse sporadically erupted, conquering the granite trails, softening their edges and bringing the grey rock to life. Olor had no idea why or when he knew this place. But as the mist cleared, an echo of a memory began to resonate. Then, like the lightning of a distant storm, something flashed and struck. Olor shivered, recognising the scene as a memory. His memory. His first memory.

'Where are we?' Olor asked Pejanen, who stood beside him.

'It is known as Gougane. A place of your youth.'

At the lakeside, Olor heard the sounds of a gentle hooting, low at first. From beneath some reeds appeared a female adult swan. Long-necked and majestic in her cleanliness, sleek and alert, waiting for safety to be established. From behind her a grey cygnet emerged, responding to her signal. It was energetic, clumsy and adventurous in its young waddle. No bigger than a hand, the little swan battled through forests of grass. Its webbed feet moving with speed, thrilled with the sound of lapping water. Olor saw the pair disappear behind a cloud of mist, and with a gentle puff of wind, a mother and child emerged from the dispersing white pall.

The boy was skinny, no more than five years old. He wore cowhide trousers, a shirt woven from thick yarn, leather armlets, and a leather waistcoat. Both sides of the boy's head were shaved, long brown platted tails at the back, clustered at the end, a line of blue woad daubed across his eyes. A pair of wooden daggers attached with leather straps to his hips.

'Olor!' called the mother. 'It's too late for a swim, you've been there all day.'

The child willfully ignored her, took off his woolen shirt and dived in. The glint of something golden on the boy's wrist caught Olor's eye. The bracelet. In his hand he held a similar bracelet. The one he had earlier dug from the floor of the hut when alone, desperately looking for answers. He wished for more answers now. As his eyes moved from the bracelet to the vision of the boy and his mother, Olor felt a wave of paralysis wash over him.

'It is the same bracelet,' said Pejanen, calmly disregarding Olor's bewilderment at the scene. 'Go closer if you wish, they can't see you.'

Olor moved closer. The boy's mother stood tall in her leathers. She was young, a mother not long out of her own childhood. Slung over her hips, she wore a belt ornately decorated, with tassels on the trim. Olor's head began to pound.

'You have 'til the sun reaches the tops of that willow, then out,' whispered Olor, to himself, his lips trembling at the words.

'You have 'til the sun reaches the tops of that willow, then out,' the mother called.

'They will arrive soon,' whispered Olor.

'They will arrive soon,' the boy shouted back, excitedly.

Olor's lips quivered. His knuckles were white from tightly holding the bracelet. Then came the sound. A far-off rhythmic hooting. The boy instinctively held his bracelet hand in the air. An outline of four birds appeared in the distance, Olor saw them to be swans. Still treading water, the boy guided the quartet of swans. The lead swan brought the others in a corkscrew circle around the lake, then straightened them up to their landing. Their webbed feet extended as they skimmed across the water, flapping to a halt.

The flock arranged themselves around the boy, shaking tail feathers and bobbing their heads. He laughed and the swans turned to the mother and bowed. She replied in kind. Seeing the sun had moved to the agreed point on the willow tree, she called on her son to bid the swans farewell.

Olor listened to the sounds of the swans whispering to the boy. Pejanen Tyger saw in Olor's face that he could understand them.

*'Olor of the lake,*
*Soon to end your days of joy,*
*Your days of draíocht,*
*The darkness comes, 'til,*
*The child of bears proclaims the dawn.'*

It was the mother who heard the sound of hooves first. Turning, she saw three gargantuan horses charging forward. Each was twenty hands high, eight-legged, with protruding canine teeth, and cold blue eyes like sapphires. On their backs, three cowled riders held the long sleek manes as reins.

The mother stood warily on the shore between the visitors and her son. The boy looked on from the middle of the lake, unable to move.

'You are on the Ullaunite lands. Dismount and present yourself,' the mother ordered.

There was no reply.

'Where do you come from? Speak, or be deemed unwelcome.'

'We need no permission to be here,' said a voice, from beneath a cowl.

'Present yourself.' The mother stiffened her back and raised her chin.

A rider dismounted. Walking slowly, his broad white bare feet made no sound on the grass. He stood looking down at her.

'Declare yourself and bend your knee, before this Ullaunite,' commanded the mother.

The rider pulled back his hood. Seeing his white dome and trim of hair, she took a step back. She pulled her returner from a sheath secreted in the belt at the small of her back. Twirling it, she presented arms. The figure standing before her had a branding on the top of his chest. A wound that wept, never to heal. The sign of a traitor - the "I" of Inimicus.

He introduced himself. 'I am Mustela.'

'I know who you are. Another step, and I'll open you, Inimicus.' She looked to see where her boy was. The swans formed a protective line in front of the child, flapping their wings aggressively. Mustela moved to take a step beyond her.

'I have not come for you,' his voice sonorous and deep.

The mother gave her final warning. 'Cease and leave this place!'

'It's not me you should be worried about. Is it Decima?' said Mustela, impassively, turning to one of the still-seated riders.

Decima raised her hand, pointing her talon-like finger at the mother.

'No,' she cried '… no.' She felt a shudder of fear and turned quickly to look at the boy. Her arms flopped to the side, instantly resigned to fate, unable to put up a fight. The power already was too strong. Her eyes glazed over and she dropped her returner. The boy in the water knew there was something dark in the air.

'Mama,' he called.

As he watched, Olor leaned into Pejanen, needing his massive size to keep him upright. He stood motionless with his hand on the fur hide of the bear, shaking like the last leaf of autumn. Olor saw the mother was paler now. Her eyes lost with a cold blue tinge around them. The swans had become agitated. He saw her walk knee-high into the lake. She moved onto all fours and plunged her head beneath the water. Her hair floated serenely like watercress. Bubbles emerged and she never raised her head again.

Olor felt like his mind was being harrowed as he saw the mother float and lose contact with the lake floor. Moments later, the rider raised her hand again. Extending four fingers, then retracting them, one by one, each swan dropped its head below the water and began to drown. The boy frantically dived to raise them but there were too many – and he was too small. He dived to submerge himself too.

'Don't go boy! The Regnum needs your oil,' called Mustela.

The cowled rider raised his hands and with an invisible magic, dragged the boy through the water toward the shore. As he did so, the mist rolled in and enveloped the scene.

Pejanen Tyger and Olor were alone in the Ullauns again surrounded by the fronds. Olor knew he had seen his own capture. The golden bracelet sat in his trembling hand.

'Why did you show me this?' Olor pleaded.

'Revelation,' answered the beast, walking away.

In the background, Olor could again hear the chasing Robusti, sniffing and searching through the vegetation. In the Ullauns again, Pejanen Tyger's immense languid stride carried him to the trees of the woodland beyond. There, his form loosened until he became shadow and disappeared. Olor began to run. The swell of fear rose again. The mob saw him break cover and went in pursuit. This time, they were certain they would run him down. And they did.

# Chapter 12

The Book of Dubhe

*Chapter 413*
*Verse 878*

*The rise of Snowdrops.*

*On the eleventh moon, and the cold star opens through the grey and I feel my head straighten and wish to lengthen, moving toward the cold burning star. My seed is still well stacked with food and nourishment for many days, for I am a child of the forest floor.*

*The eight, ninth and tenth moon I have obeyed the law of sleep and lie here waiting to rise. I hear it first before the others. When they see me rise, they knew they have survived the chill. Where I go first, others will follow. Another dark time has come to an end with this pioneer.*

*I have survived and thus you have survived.*

The darkness of Mount Bolcawn's main chamber echoed with squeals, Blacktooth gave a shoulder roll, and placed the unconscious Finn Giorra on the ground, bowing and then waiting for Mustela's reaction.

'What is this?'

'Finn Giorra, sire, Asio Clan.'

Mustela rose from his weasel throne and walked forward, his bare feet cushioned by pelts. Leaning down, he grabbed Finn by the waistcoat, lifting him up, looked at his face, verifying the Robustus' extraordinary claim. He looked to Blacktooth, partly in disbelief. 'You captured Finn Giorra?'

'I thought it would please you and the Regnum, sire.'

'Even his returners!' cooed Mustela, seeing Finn's blades slung over Blacktooth's shoulder. Mustela paused, taking time to mull over the magnitude of this achievement. Perhaps he had not seen the potential in Blacktooth before. It was a thought that distracted him, among others. 'I may have underestimated you, Blacktooth. This small thing has dispatched many a Lictor and Robustus. Yet, you alone have done what they could not. And unscathed as well.'

'He took my nose, sire.' Blacktooth raised his head to reveal the cavity, which had stopped bleeding, yet still glistened as cut flesh.

'Lucky he didn't take your throat as well.' Mustela dropped Finn to the floor. The thud woke him. 'What news of your cohort?'

Blacktooth kept his eyes to the floor. 'A part are in pursuit of Olor.' he paused. 'The rest have been despatched… by this Ullaunite.'

Mustela took a moment. With nothing but the force from his outstretched hand, he lifted Blacktooth off the ground, turning him in mid-air. He paralysed the creature's body, except for his eyes and mouth.

'Dispatched you say. However, you survive. Only you. No witness to tell of your tale.'

'No, sire.'

'How fortunate. I can tolerate clever, but I cannot abide lucky, I don't trust luck.'

The weasels squealed.

'Why did you survive?' said Mustela, with a glare.

Blacktooth could not think quickly enough in his present state, paralysis affecting his mind. He fumbled for words.

The weasels squealed again.

'He was saved because he is a coward,' called Finn, from the floor.

Weasel heads turned. All the attention went to the prone Ullaunite.

'A coward?' announced Mustela. 'Blacktooth is Robustus. Born and bred to defend the honour of the Regnum. He does not know fear, let alone cowardice, both are outside his comprehension.'

'The cohort fought as best they could,' replied Finn, 'but they were no match. I slaughtered them all.'

'You did?'

'I had assumed I'd killed them all too, but there was one coward, filled with treachery, as only the Regnum can fill.' Finn spat out the words.

'Go on,' Mustela insisted.

'Hiding beneath the bodies of his comrades. I let my guard down, sheathing my weapons.'

'And then?'

'He leapt forward and smashed my head with a rock. As I said a coward, but a clever one.'

Mustela looked again to Blacktooth and considered the scenario. 'How did you take his nose then?' he asked.

There was a pause. Blacktooth thought that the lie was about to undo them both.

'I had a chance to let my returner off before I passed out. It did its best. Took his nose, but not his throat,' said Finn.

'Clever.' Mustela said with genuine admiration in his voice. 'Cowardice! Now that's a worry. The Regnum has no place for cowards. All cowards will be replaced. Are you a coward?'

'No, sire,' replied Blacktooth

'Only when it serves the purpose of the Regnum,' interrupted Finn.

'When it serves the Regnum?' Mustela repeated, in a whisper, the weasels rolling beneath his white toes.

'The others lacked treachery and are now dead. This coward survived and returned with his prize.'

Mustela drew closer to the Ullaunite. 'Why do you defend him?'

'I do not defend him, but Ullaunites are known for the truth and their power of facing it – that is all.'

'Ah, yes, that renowned skill.' Mustela sneered. 'Yet, the ultimate destruction of your clan or my ascendency in the Ullauns … you don't seem to want to face that, do you?'

'That is not yet a truth,' said Finn, defiantly.

Mustela took a moment to consider his response. Affecting faux disinterest, he turned away.

'Assemble a new cohort and kill Olor,' he commanded, with a broad wave of his hand.

'Yes, sire,' said a relieved Blacktooth.

As Mustela walked away, he produced a vial of Anam oil from

his pocket. Finn felt a knot grow in his stomach. He had heard about them before. An amber liquid that bubbled with the power of the Ullanite soul. Magic reduced to syrup. Mustela casually tossed the vial to Blacktooth who caught it before it could hit the ground. He bowed to his master and gave Finn a confused look. The last thing Finn saw was a departing Blacktooth gulping down the contents of the vial. Before he had even left the chamber, the beast was already undergoing another gargantuan transformation.

◆    ✦    ◆

'Finn Giorra – what a prize. What a blow to the resistance.' Mustela sat on his throne, reveling in the present state of affairs. He ordered a train of weasels forward from the morass, which moved to Finn with purpose. They scampered around his wrists and arms, binding him tightly, up to his neck. 'Much has changed, Finn Giorra.'

'Not for the better,' grunted Finn.

'Oh, I would beg to differ.'

'You may beg.'

Mustela smiled. 'We are not starting off on the best of terms.'

'Good.'

The weasels twisted tighter around Finn.

'You seem to have your mind made up about me,' said Mustela.

'Your reputation precedes you,' said the squeezed Ullaunite.

'Do tell.'

'You are a disgraced Ullaunite, a traitor branded "Inimicus". Your treachery convinced others to follow your quest for power, transforming the Ullauns, from idyll into the darkness of this Regnum. You're a cannibal for the oil of your own kind, wishing to put nature beneath your control.'

'All true,' Mustela acknowledged, 'but cannibal? That's an emotive word!' Mustela raised an eyebrow and showed his teeth, sharpened and yellow. 'Many moons ago, I was like you – a foolish seed collector, a serf on the wheel. But then I found out something! All this – this Ullauns – is a fantastic waste of time. There is only power, Finn Giorra. Above beauty, above the mystic, above truth itself … power wins. Power always wins.' Mustela opened his arms with a flourish.

'You betrayed your own, and you are still a serf to the Scawl,' Finn said.

'Said like the true child of the Asio, a true seer. A sage.' Mustela laughed at the familiar accusation. 'I see Gannymeade still pours polemic in your ear. We all need a higher power, something to look up to. You have Nature, and I have the Scawl.'

The weasels tightened. Finn felt his bones bend under the stress of their grip.

Mustela wiped his black lips with bony fingers. 'Before you have power, Finn Giorra, you must have control. And control means oil. In time, I will be stronger than the Ancients that punished me, destroyed my returner, stripped me of my Anam.' Mustela ripped open his shirt, revealing the scar at the top of his chest. 'They branded me with the "I" of Inimicus. The mark of the traitor will never be erased never heal. It still weeps but I now pride myself in this mark. It is the crest of the Regnum. The symbol of rule. My rule!' Mustela thundered, adopting the stance of an orator.

'You don't rule the Asio,' wheezed Finn, as he began to turn blue. 'You will be defeated.'

Mustela laughed. 'I doubt it. The Regnum is unceasing, relentless. I have fashioned it so. You? You only have stories. The Ursine, the child born of Ancient Bears – the one who will save you. I doubt that story very much.' Mustela sniffed.

'But enough of this.' A smile scampered across his mouth, 'let us now to our work.'

Behind him, a cave wall rolled open and a cohort of Lictors emerged. They approached the still bound Finn and dragged him behind Mustela who had been spirited forward on a dais of weasels. Beyond the door was a chamber filled with the sound of pistons and mechanics.

'Would you like to see my trophy cabinet?' asked Mustela, delighting in his own wordplay. 'This is Finn Giorra,' he grandiosely announced, to his lackeys. 'His Anam oil alone will keep us in power for countless of eternities. Brimful, this one.'

Inside the chamber, blue and yellow lights flickered on to illuminate rows of circular glass tanks on stands. Distributed in all directions, rows of curved glass filling the cavern. Finn began to lose consciousness, the blood to his head being pinched a bit too tightly.

'Loosen your grip!' he whispered.

Mustela replied with a nod. The weasels did as their master commanded. The colour returned to Finn's face. He was carried past a line of glass tanks on either side of a walkway. Each tank three meters high. Mustela turned and caught sight of his contorted reflection on the curved glass, he reached out to touch his own face and waited a moment, blinking at his own reflection.

'You are peculiar for an Ullaunite,' Mustela observed, as he considered his image. 'You appear resigned to your fate. Have you no fight left?'

'Where will you kill me?' asked Finn.

'Oh, I'm not going to kill you,' replied an amused Mustela. ' I need you alive. You can't milk a dead cow, can you?'

Finn's awareness had begun to sharpen. His eyes were adjusting to the light in the chamber. He could clearly see the contents of the tanks. In one, was a figure suspended in a clear blue liquid: an old man stripped to undergarments. His eyes were bound with bandages, his head tilted. Needle puncturing the skin, busy with extraction. Finn could not make out how long the space was, but as far as his eyes could see, there were rows and rows of these tanks. All contained suspended and tubed-up Ullaunites, bathing in grotesque industrial stasis.

'I have thousands of such places all over the Ullauns,' smiled Mustela. 'My oilfields as it were.'

To Finn's left, were two tanks in total darkness. Mustela signaled to one of his Robusti guards who nodded and reached to a bank of switches on the wall. Lights flickered and then fully illuminated the first tank. There she was. Suspended like the others, bare feet, piped and bound. Twitching faintly. Ashket. Finn's sister. Finn's eyelids were growing heavy and he began to breathe deep and low.

'Doesn't she look well?' Mustela proffered. 'By the way, the jerking is nothing to worry about,' he said. 'It is just the body getting used to the process. It passes. Like all things it passes.'

The last tank lit up. Filled with a blue liquid, two pipes with pins. It was empty.

'Your carriage awaits.' Mustela pointed to the tank with a flourish. With a gentle open hand to Finn's forehead, Mustela put him to sleep. The Ullaunite fell limp in the arms of the Lictors. Sensing his lack of consciousness, the weasels let him go and scampered off to rejoin the dais beneath Mustela. Within minutes, Finn was stripped of all but his armlets, in his undergarments, bandaged, piped and suspended in the tank, beside his sister.

'Welcome to the Regnum,' whispered Mustela, as the first pump whizzed into life. 'Now sleep and give me as much oil as you can.'

Finn's extraction had begun.

# Chapter 13

The Book of Merak

*Chapter 63*
*Verse 4*

*Mice climbing a stem of barley*

*After the fourth moon, the meadow stalks begin to bend with heavy seed. We see the strain and know what will and what will not take our weight. A fear swells with our hunger and its symmetry of consequence cannot be explained in words. To climb the stalk is to be seen by the kite above. To strive toward life and food is to strive toward death, such is the symmetry of consequence.*

The firmness of the pillow was not to her liking. Boudicca lay on top of Ashket's bed. It was quite a bit smaller than her own, so her feet spilled out over the end. She had read the little book in her locket for a while. It wasn't long before her eyes began to feel heavy, and close. She drifted off to the hinterland of half-sleep – the place where one feels awake but the mind loosens its moorings from the body, wishing to be pulled away by seismic undertows.

Just then she smelled smoke. Sniffing at first and then seeing it come through the cracks in the door. Anxiously, she got up and opened the door to find the common area inside Cumann rock engulfed in flames – fire trailing up the walls – the books of the Omnium Gatherum ablaze. She was just about to call, when she saw a figure appear from one of the corridors. It was a girl in Ul-launite leathers, two returners on her hips. She was unknown to Boudicca. The girl was in her mid-teens, dark hair tied back. Boudicca saw her go to the coat of arms that hung on the wall of the chamber and pressed her hand against a rock. A secret drawer opened and quickly the girl took out seven returners that were stored there. From the same drawer the girl took out seven of the small books that were similar to the one Boudicca had found in the locket. The girl placed the books into the hilts of the returners. All except for one, which she looked at for a moment. The girl put her hand into her top and took out a locket that hung around her neck. Boudicca recognised it immediately and took out the locket on her own neck and saw them to be the same. The girl placed the last book into the locket and discretely hid it, before being joined by another figure who appeared jumping through the flames.

It was Gannymeade, who was now half her present age. Not as plump or as grey. 'Are they all here?' the young Gannymeade asked.

The girl nodded without looking at her.

'These returners will not return,' said Gannymeade. 'It is now for you to throw them and they will be dispersed to the far-reaches of any world they choose. This will be your secret.'

The girl looked at the returners without replying, and seemed consumed by the task.

'Do you understand Sarah?' asked Gannymeade. 'We must survive. Mustela cannot get the Children of Bears. It will be the end of days, if he does.'

Boudicca then realised Gannymeade was talking to her mother, as a young girl.

Sarah nodded and quickly threw the returners, one by one, in quick succession toward the roof of the chamber. An opening appeared and they flew off into the moonlit night.

'We must join the others to repel the Robusti attack,' said Gannymeade, as she exited through the flames.

Sarah gave a broken-smiled look to Boudicca and placed her hand on the locket that hung around her neck. Boudicca did the same. Sarah turned and ran after Gannymeade into the flames. A column of books collapsed, and feeling the heat Boudicca closed her eyes.

◆        ✦        ◆

A sound woke her. Boudicca sat up, wiped her eyes and gingerly got out of Ashket's bed. Feeling nauseous she tried to abate it by putting her hand on the locket around her neck. She made her way outside. The chamber was no longer in flames and was cold and dark save for the flames from the dying fire in the middle of the Cumann.

A figure sat there, looking into the dancing fire flames. It turned, and revealed Gannymeade, puffing on her pipe quietly. 'She visited you, did she?'

Boudicca nodded as she moved into the light.

'We are nearing the end,' said Gannymeade. 'The forces at play are too great for me to control. The dark hour of the Regnum is almost upon us.'

Boudicca said nothing and looked at her plaintively.

There was a long pause. 'As a child, I was always adventurous. Sticking my nose in where it was not safe to do so. I fell into a well once. Very deep. Very cold. Very dark,' said Gannymeade, as her eyes devoured the fire light. 'I spent the night there, my strength waning. I was holding onto the root of a tree. I wished to sleep and I fought as best I could, and the only thing that kept me awake was the fear ....' Gannymeade wiped her mouth with her sleeve '... the fear,' she whispered to herself. 'I was just about to let go, to drown and pay dearly for my curiosity and then I heard it.' A brief smile flashed across Gannymeade's mouth. 'My mother's voice calling me. Mothers give life and save lives.' She paused in her story. 'I am fearful again,' said Gannymeade.

Boudicca did nothing but look to the fire herself.

Gannymeade's gold chain dancing from her nose to her ear. 'In your face I see the markings of your mother,' said Gannymeade. 'Your mother was a messenger of the bears.'

'Markings?' said a confused Boudicca. 'I have no scars.'

'They are not scars, child,' replied Gannymeade, weakly, 'they are a constellation that is written on your face.'

Boudicca was a little confused.

'I fear I'm not worthy of the role which I now occupy,' said Gannymeade, somberly.

Boudicca looked to the pot, ladle and cup, which sat beside the fire. She picked up the cup and ladled it full. 'Your fear saved your life once. Trust it again,' said Boudicca.

Boudicca offered the cup to Gannymeade, who looked at her strangely. 'Juniper tea?' said Boudicca. 'A magical brew.'

Gannymeade took the cup, gulped from it and smiled with calmer eyes. 'You must find your mother. Our very existence depends on it.' Gannymeade extended her left hand to shake.

Boudicca ignored it, hugging her warmly instead. They pulled away from each other.

'Constantina. Tarquin.' Gannymeade called to the shadows.

A cloaked Constantina walked into the light, as did Tarquin, his knapsack on his back.

'Constantina is your guide. She is the only one who has been to the centre of Mount Bolcawn and returned alive. There will be problems on the way. Use Tarquin as your problem solver.' Gannymeade smiled at them. The matriarch got to her feet and looked at each one intently. 'Your journey is dangerous. Mount Bolcawn is protected on all sides. There are many Robusti. I have engaged another to help you at this point.'

'Who?' pressed Boudicca.

'A creature called, Tullikepu,' said Gannymeade.

Tarquin gave Constantina a look at the mention of the creature's name. Constantina looked ahead, ignoring his attention.

'Beyond the Robusti, you enter the caves, where the Lloyb and the Gegoyn live. Next you will face Mustela and his Praetorian guard, Decima. She is a warrior, gifted with the dark magic of The Scawl. In truth, your return is not assured, so say your goodbyes now, Boudicca,' warned Gannymeade.

'To whom?'

'Your grandparents.'

Boudicca understood and nodded.

Outside stood the Fia with the white stipe on his head, two other deer waited for Tarquin and Constantina. Boudicca's mount lowered his head and she climbed up holding the antlers for balance. Gannymeade was surprised by her mounting technique.

'Go and find her, Boudicca Moriarty,' the matriarch said.

Gannymeade stood between Constantina and Tarquin, they placed their hands into hers and held them there. 'Wait at the cave and help will come,' Gannymeade advised, letting their hands go forlornly. She looked to Constantina. 'Give him as much as you can.'

Constantina nodded.

'We will send a signal for reinforcements when the battle starts,' said Tarquin.

'Look to the skies, Gannymeade,' said Constantina.

Gannymeade nodded at their ambition and stepped back from the Fia. 'Somniate Sine Metu,' she said.

'Somnia Sine Metu,' said the group in unison.

The trio bolted through the shadows on their Fia. They made straight for Prospero and Nonie's house arriving under the safe cover of darkness. Boudicca gently pushed open the door of her grandparent's bedroom. Both were fast asleep. She wished to wake them but held back on the urge. Instead, she remembered their love and kindness. Maurice Fitzgerald sat at the end of the bed; his eyes peered through the half-dark. He twitched an ear, and continued to stare. Boudicca knew Maurice would calm them in her absence.

'Bye, Maurice,' Boudicca whispered, as she stroked him to a light purr.

Going to her own room, she took out the book from her locket. More pages had become clear. She returned it to its locket and placed it around her neck again. Outside Constantina and Tarquin waited in the moonlight. Boudicca climbed out her window and mounted her Fia.

'Are you done?' asked Constantina.

Boudicca nodded and said, 'Let us reclaim our loved ones.' She turned the Fia with a pull of his mane and galloped off, side-by-side. They approached the forest and became one with the shadows.

# Chapter 14

The Book of Dubhe

*Chapter 1040*
*Verse 3*

*On cats and their leisure.*

*When the night star waxes, I care not for moons and stars and the celeste, and what others think and what I think, for I am at rest and no travail troubles me.*

*My nature dictates my needs and I am king and all around is either Christendom or serf. No doubt all serve me, the small are my nourishment, the grand are my amusement. The spheres in the darkness perform their music for my leisure.*

*Oh, Graymalkin, 'tis a fine secret to know.*

On the back of the Fia, she heard and felt the thud of the hooves beneath.

When the hooves ceased to churn the yielding forest floor, the three Ullaunites decided to continue on foot. After dismounting, the Fia left impersonally – except Boudicca's deer, which seemed reluctant to leave. Boudicca gently shooed it away. After a moment's hesitation it turned and ran to join the others.

'It's very rare for a Fia to form a bond with its rider,' said Tarquin.

Constantina agreed.

They walked for a short time, deeper into the forest, following natural signposts only known to the Ullaunites. These led to the cave where they could rest, take on sustenance and wait. The cave was wide and cavernous at the opening, but the further back it went, it reached a pinch-point at the end.

As they sat, tucking away rations, Constantina wondered as

to what to do next. Mount Bolcawn was a monumental challenge and much had changed since she'd entered the mountain many moons ago. It had been fortified and the prospect made her nervous.

'All we can do now is wait, as instructed,' said Tarquin, just to fill the silence after eating.

They waited, comforting themselves by looking at the stars in the sky.

'It is said that the Robusti are also the cities in which they live. That their buildings are made of the beasts themselves -- each Robustus a living brick. Is this true?' asked Tarquin.

'Yes,' confirmed Constantina, 'and the closer you get to the mountain the bigger, stronger and quicker those Robusti become. Their cities can breathe and move to defend themselves.'

'They get bigger!' said Boudicca.

'I'd rather be an Ullaunite than a Robustus any moon,' said Tarquin, boosting his own confidence.

'If we get past them, then we face the Chamber of Lloyb,' said Constantina.

'What are the Lloyb?' Boudicca enquired. She'd heard mention of them earlier.

'The Lloyb are as prodigious as Robusti – numbering in their millions – but are only powerful beneath the mountain. Two and a half feet tall, huge eyes, the empty shells of former Ullaunites, crazed, wild and wretched things. While they are blind and fearful of the light, even the forces of the Regnum will not venture beneath the mountain. They are to be pitied – but only from afar,' warned Constantina, stretching her neck at the thought of the trials.

Boudicca broke the uneasy silence. 'Why did you go to the centre of the mountain before?'

'Many moons ago, I went with a party to save some Ullaunites, who had been taken. We suffered losses, but got through the Robusti. Only I survived the Lloyd. The rest were … lost.' Constantina cleared her throat and announced, 'We must wait here, as Gannymeade ordered.'

They all nodded, happy to change the subject with more silence.

Boudicca heard something move outside the cave.

'Constantina,' whispered Boudicca, pointing to the darkness.

Constantina got to her feet and clicked out to the forest.

'What is it?' whispered Tarquin. His hand covered his returner.

Boudicca did the same. 'There's something out there.'

'Something?' asked Tarquin.

The group moved out of the cave and into the moonlight. Constantina's brow knitted in concentration, poised and ready.

'I see the sounds but I cannot find the source.' She unsheathed her returners from their position on her back.

'Robusti?' asked Boudicca.

Constantina shook her head and continued clicking in all directions. 'Whatever it is … it's gone,' she announced, warily.

'Gone? Gone where?' Tarquin quizzed, scanning the forest with peeled eyes.

'Here,' said a voice, from behind them.

They all turned to the cave behind to find a recognisable creature sitting contentedly on a rock. It was a fox. Its hair was not the usual red, but a shading of silver, darker on the shoulder, back, and head. Light hair on the chest and the tip of its tail. It looked malnourished, its pelt riddled with mange. Parts of its skin were visible through its fur. There were blisters on its lips and black teeth in its mouth. Its eyes were drowsy and intoxicated with weakness. The Ullaunites maintained their weapons at the ready.

'Declare yourself,' ordered Constantina.

The animal got to his feet and gave a stretch, trying to hide its shaking legs. 'Oh, please, you know who I am,' he said, coyly, slurring a little.

Constantina remained silent and motionless, pressing the animal to answer the question.

'My name is, Tullikepu.'

Boudicca repeated his name out loud.

'An Ancient name,' said Tarquin.

'Ancient? Oh, I'm older than that.'

'A fox,' said Boudicca, marveling at the creature.

'I am not a fox, child, I am a Downcha!'

'An ancient animal,' said Tarquin, 'a precursor.'

'We are …' began Constantina.

'I know who you are …' the Downcha cut in, smiling, 'because Gannymeade sent for me.'

'Your friends are in that Mountain.' He turned to Boudicca, 'And you are the daughter of Sarah Moriarty. What company I entertain?' The Downcha looked at her face in its entirety.

'Do you know her?' asked Boudicca.

'She blazed a trail even with us ancients. You have the markings,' said the creature. This was the second time this had been said to Boudicca. 'What markings?' asked Boudicca, abruptly.

'That is for me to know and for you to find out, but now your mother is in the clutches of the Regnum. And you need my help.'

'Help us then!' implored Boudicca.

'I will. But as you know, nothing in this, or any life, is free,' replied Tullikepu. 'There is a price.'

'What? I will pay it,' said Boudicca.

'It may not be for you to pay child. I can take you to the entrance of the Chamber of Lloyb.' Tullikepu looked in the direction toward Mount Bolcawn. 'There are hundreds of thousands of Robusti that surround the Mountain.'

'How will we get past them?' asked Tarquin, wary of the answer.

Tullikepu smiled, 'Good question Ullaunite. How will we do this?' Tullikepu turned to Constantina. 'Well Constantina?'

'We are going to walk straight through them,' replied Constantina, looking toward the mountain.

There was a silence. Boudicca and Tarquin were expecting another part to the plan, but the next line was not forthcoming.

'Constantina?' enquired a worried Boudicca

'The Downcha is an ancient animal, capable of much magic in their time, but the Regnum reduced them to their present station, extracting all their Anam oil. They are but animals now with no magic, only memories of magic,' said Constantina.

'Yes.' The Downcha smiled, his eyes locked on the senior Ullaunite.

'We will be overrun,' said Tarquin.

'Yes, we will if we are seen,' said Tullikepu.

The Downcha moved from the rock to the ground. 'The art of being unseen is something that has been lost in us. We don't have the oil anymore,' said Tullikepu, 'but if we had the oil, so many things would be possible. It's like having a key and not having a door to open.'

'Take my oil, whatever I have,' said a rushed Boudicca.

'I'm afraid child you live in the world of the seen. For my magic to work, I need the oil from one who lives in the world of the unseen. The world of the blind,' said Tullikepu.

He turned his head to Constantina.

'You will drain her,' said Tarquin.

'Tarquin,' said Constantina, calming him with an open hand, 'it's ok.'

'Come, Constantina,' said Tullikepu.

Constantina moved forward.

'Grab my tail,' urged the Downcha.

Constantina grabbed his tail with her hand. To Boudicca's amazement, the blind Ullaunite and the Downcha took on a translucent quality as a shaft of moonlight passed through them. A moment later they disappeared, becoming completely invisible. Immediately they returned, with a little swish of the Dowcha's tail. Constantina looked shaken after the experience and Tarquin knew it had taken a lot out of her.

Rejuvenated by the experience and more energetic than before, Tullikepu smiled. 'Now, that is a fine trade,' he announced.

Boudicca went to Constantina and was stopped short with an open hand.

'I'm fine Boudicca,' she smiled.

'That is but a moment, with one,' said Tarquin. 'What about the two of us as well?'

'Well then you best hope she has enough in reserve.' The Downcha smiled.

'I do. Let us go,' said Constantina.

'That's the spirit!' said Tullikepu. 'That is how we will walk through them.'

'I hope this works,' said Constantina.

'Me too, for if it does not …' said Tullikepu, with a smile, 'we will surely join the ranks of the dead.'

# Chapter 15

The Book of Merak

*Chapter 829*

*Verse 577*

*On wolves and the light*

*The moon rises at the half day. We know it will shine later and when all is slow and sleepy, it will be above, basking in its own glow.*

*Then we will open our throats and straighten our spines, so we may howl the song that lies silent in our blood. The moon's bright light full in our eyes before the hunt, the verse followed by the lines, our song will be broken in to these parts.*

They gulped juniper tea by the mugful. Some bit their fingernails. Others cleared their throats, more through a nervous tic than need. Upon learning that a group of their comrades had left Cumann Rock, none dared look each other in the eye. They just stared at the flames of the fire in front of them, wishing the crackling wood to deliver news of their friends and family. Gannymeade ladled tea generously into mugs that shook in worried hands.

Ithaca Pipistrelle sat the most affected. Never had he been so long without his sister. His blind eyes bounced firelight back to its source. His thirst for tea unrelenting. He rubbed and rolled his hands searching the crevices of his own fingers and wrist, as if looking for traces of sense and memory.

'Drink up, Ithaca,' said Gannymeade. 'It will calm you.'

'She's never been so far away.' He began to click to himself, a private prayer for his sister's safekeeping and return. 'How did I not wake? Did she spell me?' he asked, no one in particular.

'She didn't spell you,' said Gannymeade, 'you slept is all.'

He clicked again, looking up at the group. 'Did she spell me, do you think?'

'They have gone to Mount Bolcawn,' reiterated Gannymeade. Ithaca continued to whisper to himself.

'They will signal us when they need us,' said Tycho.

Ithaca clicked his private mantra. Both Sciurus sisters tried to calm themselves, feeling emotion swell inside.

'We have to help them,' Alba affirmed out loud.

'But we are the only Ullaunites left,' her sister replied.

'The greater onus is upon us then,' Alba said

Niamh acknowledged the point with a silent nod. Sensing the growing disquiet, Gannymeade felt the need to speak.

'We need to wait for their signal,' repeated Gannymeade.

'That is hesitation,' said Alba.

'It is making sure that our next step is the correct one,' replied Gannymeade, firmly.

Behind Gannymeade came the sound of sniffling. Old Joe Martes was standing there, his hands by his side, a much older man now, like a thousand moons had passed over him in the hours since he was last seen.

'Come. Drink some tea,' whispered Tycho.

'It's me,' said Joe. 'I am that one who has betrayed you.'

All eyes turned to him instantly.

'What are you saying?' asked Gannymeade, holding up an open hand to pacify the group. She passed him some tea.

Joe's cracked lips went to the cup but he stopped it before he supped. 'I have betrayed Finn and now the others, including my son,' he mumbled. 'Mustela came to me in a dream,' said Joe, his face gaunt and his eyes twitched with fear like the hunted or birds.

'How do you know this?' asked Tycho.

'He found my weakness, Tycho.'

'What weakness?'

'Isha,' said Joe, his lips quivering, 'my wife …' his voice meandered off.

'But she is …' Tycho paused. 'It has been some years now Joe.'

'I know, Tycho.'

Old Joe took a moment to recompose himself. 'One night, as

we were collecting seed, I found myself thinking of Isha. It had hardly occurred, when out of nowhere she appeared right before my eyes. Mustela conjured her. He used my grief as a key to unlock me.'

'Does he have such powers?' Tycho looked to Gannymeade.

'With the Scawl anything is possible.' Gannymeade piteously looked to Old Joe.

'He came to me, Gannymeade. Told me I could meet her again.' His voice was barely a whisper.

'Joe …' Gannymeade moved forward, sensing what he might say next.

'Even though she is gone,' said Old Joe, 'my love grows every day, and that is the saddest thing, don't you think?'

The young Ullaunites were confused, unsure of the mixture of guilt and innocence.

'Isha got me to view your ancient seed locations, I joined you in your dreams and I told Isha where the Ullaunites would be. That was the agreement with Mustela.'

The group gasped.

'Inimicus,' said Niamh.

'Hold your tongue, Niamh Sciurus,' hissed Tycho.

'He betrayed us. He said so himself.'

'This man fought battles to save our kind before you were born. Respect that,' said Tycho.

Niamh sat down.

The fire reacted to Tycho's energy, a swirling flame rising into the air.

'I am sorry,' Joe began, getting lost in his words, his head moving from side-to-side, 'I am Inimicus.' Looking around with desperate eyes, he cut a lost and broken figure. 'I put my boy in harm's way through my own loneliness.'

Gannymeade's shoulders bowed beneath the weight of another problem. 'And so it is,' she said.

'I know the penalty,' Joe looked deeply into the fire.

Tycho was angered by Joe's words.

'Stop now Joe,' said Tycho. 'Don't say it! Have some tea, reconsider, take a moment.' Tycho made for the ladle.

'Our code demands a punishment,' said Joe, his eyes were

plaintive and mournful.

'Consider again. I beg of you.' Tycho's voice was trembling.

'I request The Sopor – I request Tycho Asio to perform it,' he declared, to the assembly.

Gannymeade's head lowered as did Tycho's. The young Ullaunites stood looking at one another with puzzled expressions.

Gannymeade explained that Joe was demanding Tycho to perform his execution. It was a quick mercy ritual. An Ullaunite who requested The Sopor could not be denied. Execution could only be conducted by another Ullaunite. The chosen executioner could not refuse. Joe would stand in front of Tycho, who would place his hand on Joe's back, directly behind his heart. Tycho would dispatch his returner. The returning weapon would naturally find the hand of its owner, but in doing so, would pierce Joe's chest and heart. It would kill quickly. A quiet mercy. According to beliefs, the dead Ullaunite would be borne away by the Boreal winds to the Nav, joining others who have gone before.

Old Joe's breath steamed in the moonlight. 'I am responsible for the disappearance of five Ullaunites.' Joe called out, 'I call on the Ancients to witness Tycho Asio, to perform The Sopor. I beg forgiveness from all and the Bradán.' He made for the woods outside.

The others followed mesmerised by what was unfolding.

'Stand there,' ordered Tycho, looking to a spot on the ground.

Old Joe's breath quickened. His returner sensed his distress. It shook in its sheath, but Joe calmed it with a touch.

Tycho readied himself behind Joe's shoulders. He remembered standing on those very same shoulders as a boy plucking apples from trees in the Varimill forest of the Ullauns, before age had changed them. Tycho placed his hand on Joe's back, feeling the pulse of his fast-beating heart. Joe closed his eyes. Tycho threw his returner hard into the distance, dropping immediately to one knee but leaving his hand on Joe's back. The sound of the whirring blade filled the night air, reached its apex and then began to return.

Gannymeade suddenly heard the sound of clicking and quickly turned her head. She saw Ithaca place his hand on his returner, gauging the distance and speed of the onrushing blade. With the swiftest of movements and an accuracy unseen by her before, Ithaca threw his returner. It connected with Tycho's returner, deflecting it, resulting in a shower of sparks. Tycho's weapon flew past nicking Joe's shoulder. Tycho stood up and received his own weapon, once it had returned. He found Ithaca looking at him, with his own returner sitting snuggly in his hand.

'It is bad jinn to interrupt The Sopor. You could be cursed!' said Tycho, annoyed, yet equally relieved.

Ithaca took a moment and stepped forward. 'My sister is one of those fighting in that Mountain,' he began, addressing the group. 'We need as many Ullaunites as we can to get them back. I will not sit idly by, as one of our own invites Boreal winds to bear him away, because of a tradition.' Ithaca turned to Old Joe, 'If you wish to die, then do so fighting The Regnum, and if you survive that, and your wish is the same then come back here and I will finish the job. We need all Ullaunites to fight for her – including you, Joe.'

Ithaca's clarity impressed and made Gannymeade smile.

'My sister is not dead. She is alive and I will fight with all I have to keep her thus.'

'Yes!' Alba joyously punched the air.

'Gannymeade says for us to await their signal, and I believe this signal will come,' said Ithaca. With a few clicks, he turned and walked back to Cumann Rock. The rest followed.

Tycho and Gannymeade stood back and looked on as the young Ullaunites led Old Joe away with care.

'You are aware that a Sopor has never been denied,' Tycho reminded her.

'These are strange times, Tycho,' she replied, patting him on the shoulder. 'One thing is certain: they are a rare bunch of Ullaunites.'

'Lions dressed as lambs,' said Tycho.

'Lions dressed as lambs, indeed.' Gannymeade smiled.

# Chapter 16

The Book of Alkaid

*Chapter 888*
*Verse 76*

*On the making of a web*

*There is a bell I hear. I hear a bell. And there is the space be-*
*tween things; I see it before it knows itself. I lay the anchor points,*
*setting there a frame of threads. Radii to the middle stand and*
*the threads are taut. I skip along my confident work. I check the*
*spokes to see if there are enough, adding extra where needed. Once*
*strong, I tighten them and then I rest and within my gut I sum-*
*mon a holding gossamer. I weave and I spin, and I hold tight the*
*centre. Then I wait. I wait for tiny innocence to arrive and when*
*it does, it will stick fast and I will feast. For there is a bell I hear. I*
*hear a bell. They do not hear a bell.*

Boudicca could smell the must of decaying earth beneath her.

Making their way to the prow of the hill, the trio lay flat on
their stomachs – the loam, dry to the touch and soft on their bellies. Inching their heads up, they could see an expanse of brutish civilisation sprawling out over denuded lands, lying between
them and Mount Bolcawn. The walls, cloisters and lookout towers
were all made of one thing, one creature. Every hairy brick made
of Robusti, locked together from the ground up. A Robust-opolis.

The architecture was flattened and rigid, interlocking with
powerful wrists and ankles. It palpitated with the shallow breathing of barely inflated lungs. Some of the buildings were three and
four stories high, walls that separated space and defined limits.
This camp was a marvel of ingenuity and dark repression. For
some reason, they reminded Boudicca of the frozen chickens that

she saw in supermarket fridges.

The young Ullaunites and the Downcha, Tullikepu, scanned the landscape looking for a clear passage through the camp. The enormity of the task dawned on them. Tarquin swallowed whatever spit was left in his mouth. Constantina was motionless, clicking low, communicating as much disbelief as a click could. Boudicca scanned the vista with intent, quelling her fear.

'I see a path,' she whispered, and then turned to the others, 'let's go.'

They nodded, hands reaching out and accessing the invisibility through Tullikepu's tail. Though unseen, they could still see each other, albeit with a shimmering look to their appearance, as if under water. Their hair floated, their eyes widened, the edges of their garments flowed after them. This was ancient magic. They moved forward slowly.

Down they went, zigzagging their way along a descent. All the while, they kept their hands on Tullikepu, making sure they did not touch the living wall and awaken a city. They chose their steps carefully, yet a rock dislodged beneath one of their feet and tumbled noisily ahead of them. Everyone stopped. A group of Robusti briefly raised their heads, but their interest waned when sound and picture did not connect. The group continued gingerly.

The sound of sniffing followed them like a slow-moving wave. It was the sound of keen Robusti, alert to a mighty quantity of nearby Anam. Though unable to see it, the animal in them trusted their noses. Woken from their sleep – restless, agitated and on edge – Robusti tempers visibly frayed as their invisible hunger grew, the invisible feast silently walked amongst them. Teeth bared at one another, their canines snapping. Boudicca, Tarquin and Constantina barely breathed for fear of being found out.

Without warning, a Lictor – judging by its immense size – walked in front of them. No one moved. Instinctively, they reached to put their hands over their returners. The creature stopped inches from where they stood. They could smell the rotten flesh that barely clung to a blackened bone he held in its his hand, probably found in some dank midden heap. The slither of flesh proved too hard for him to ignore, but too difficult to reach with his big canines. They watched as the beast gnawed and investigated the bone's crevices, and growing apoplectic with rage. Eventually, the Lictor gave up and tossed the bone to the side. It landed in front of Boudicca's small foot.

The colossal creature loped off, then stopped, sniffing the air intently. The tension suddenly ratcheted up a notch. One false move and they would be discovered. Again, the group froze, returners at the ready. A look flashed between Boudicca and Tarquin. The Lictor sniffed. He could smell Anam oil. His gaze was drawn to the Ullaunites. They could see its teeth and wet lolling tongue in the moonlight, but it could not see them.

'Anam,' the Lictor growled, homing in on the intoxicating aroma.

Just then, a fight started between two of the Lictor's mob, drawing his attention and presence away. Boudicca, Tarquin and Constantina quickly moved on with the Downcha. Their thumping hearts returning from their mouths back to their chests.

Further on, at the edge of another Robusti mob, a Lictor – called Jeybor – stood tall. His spiked hair amplified his most dominant feature: a scar that travelled the length of his face. The scarred skin shone and was uneven – a reminder of his day as a Mung, when he stumbled across the wrong Robustus and his face became a meal, before eventually escaping. Jeybor sensed a ripple of excitement growing across the camp. There was something definitely out there. Even with his experienced eyes, Jeybor could still see nothing out of the ordinary. But he was limited by his ground-level view.

'Steps!' he barked, as he moved forward.

Robusti minions responded immediately and feverishly organised themselves into a stairwell. Jeybor climbed it without breaking stride, stopping at a height where he could survey the entire scene. Bones creaked and joints popped under his weight. He noticed that most of the Robusti excitement centered on a roadway leading toward Mount Bolcawn. Vast tracts of flesh either side, however, remained unaffected. This source of consternation seemed to grow in a straight line. 'Good,' he thought, 'straight lines are predictable.' His eyes continued to focus on a far-off rock that led to the base of Mount Bolcawn. Jeybor held his gaze, awaiting an apparition. Waiting for a mistake.

The three Ullaunites and Tullikepu continued their way through the Robustopolis. They began their ascent of a rocky incline where the footing underneath became more loose, pointed and unsteady. Nearing the top of the incline, Boudicca stepped on a rock that looked secure but gave way instantly beneath her weaker foot. She lost her footing, taking a tuft of hair from Tullikepu's tail as she toppled helplessly. He felt Boudicca's touch desert him and knew she was now visible.

'Boudicca,' Tarquin whispered.

She tried to regain her balance, but her small foot found it hard to gain purchase.

'Grab my tail,' Tullikepu called, 'or we are all gone.'

Desperately, Boudicca swung her arm and grabbed the tail. Holding herself there, she managed to regain her footing and invisibility again. Tullikepu looked over his shoulder and sensed that there was no change in the mob. The brief glimpse of Boudicca was long enough and good enough for Jeybor, whose keen eyes saw the child's figure appear and disappear.

He immediately called his cohort to give chase.

'Anam!' he shouted.

Excited by his command, the Robusti eagerly followed the pointing of his finger toward the far-off ridge.

'Here they come,' cried a fearful Tarquin.

'We must get you to the Chamber of the Lloyb, they will not go there,' said Tullikepu.

'Do not despatch your returners,' affirmed a visibly weakened Constantina, black rings around her eyes. 'It will give away your position as it returns. No weapons released.'

They began to climb higher along the ridge, digging in their feet and hands, eventually reaching the track that led along the mountain's edge. The Robusti had already caught up and vigorously attacked without being able to see the group. They tried to block the group's way, positioning themselves to pounce from the high rocks that flanked the road.

'To the tall rocks!' shouted Tullikepu, knowing that the chamber entrance lay beneath them.

The Robusti could hear the pit-pat of the Ullaunite shoes on the rocks. Sensing the movement, they readied themselves in ambush.

Ahead of him, Tarquin saw five Robusti perched on a ledge. Running scared and watching them lunge, Tarquin lost concentration and released his returner, killing the five in flight. The remaining Robusti looked at the weapon whizzing through the air, aware that it would eventually return to its Ullaunite owner and reveal their position.

'Don't catch it, Tarquin, or we are goners,' said Constantina, her shoulders slumped now with the Anam oil being drained from her by Tullikepu.

Tarquin knew he had made a mistake. An Ullaunite's returner would search endlessly until it found its owner.

'Dampen your instinct,' said Constantina.

The blade whistled through the air, frantically searching its master's hand. Without it, Tarquin knew he would grow weaker and would be prone to attack. Against all his instincts, he pulled his hand down and held it by his side. Boudicca looked at him. He smiled at her pathetically. His face was pale and wrinkling, showing more age than it had done before. Darkness shaded his eyes, too, as he returned his hand to his hip.

The Robusti looked and waited.

The four continued through a gorge, bobbing and weaving invisibly through a crazed mob. The wily Tullikepu plotting their route. Robusti blindly lunging at sounds.

With the mob fast approaching, they made for an outcropping of thin boulders, standing out like the quills of a hedgehog. Below it was a dark entrance into the belly of the mountain. They reached it and stopped at the entrance.

'Anam, Anam, Anam,' the mob chanted.

'I can go no further,' said Tullikepu, watchful of his pursuers.

The three Ullaunites let go of the creature. Constantina collapsed, as did Tarquin, both weakened from the experience for different reasons.

Tullikepu looked spritelier and with greater energy, there was a sheen to his coat, his mange had disappeared, the blisters on his mouth had cleared up. He cast his eye along the lines of his own body and approved.

'That Anam oil feels good,' he said, to himself. 'Very good, indeed. Oh, the memory of ' He looked to the two Ullaunites who were weakened and then to Boudicca who stood near them. 'A pleasure doing business.' Tullikepu disappeared and they never saw him again

•       +       •

Tarquin was weak now. He lay slumped on the ground where Boudicca held him. A horde of Robusti appeared at the cave entrance, frustrated by the tantalising proximity of their prey. Constantina was weakened, too, but she got to her hands and knees to be near Tarquin. Tarquin was wheezing and wan.

'What's wrong with him?' asked Boudicca.

'An Ullaunite is weak without their returner,' said Constantina. 'Without it he is only half of himself. Slower and less powerful. He is a delicate soul,' she said, clicking into the darkness behind.

'What will happen? Will he die?'

'I can't say. But his chances of survival are much better with his returner.'

Boudicca looked into Tarquin's face. His eyes were wild and rolling, growing more bloodshot by the moment. His lips were visibly drying.

'We must retrieve it,' exclaimed Boudicca.

'No, we are not invisible Boudicca now. We cannot leave,' said Constantina, regathering her strength. 'Returners only obey the command of the Ullaunite to whom it has been granted. If he can't get it, then no one can.'

Boudicca saw that he was now almost unconscious. 'Tarquin,' she called.

The pair could hear the returner whirring about, getting weaker and as it spun, knocking against rocks, struck and chipped by Robusti, one of whom almost caught it. The mob was rolling over each other trying to grab the prized Ullaunite weapon.

Constantina lifted Tarquin and gave him assistance. His breathing had become more laboured.

'I can get it,' said Boudicca, rising to her feet, her face determined.

'What are you doing?' asked Constantina. 'There are too many....'

Boudicca walked out in full sight of the massed horde of Robusti. To prepare for her imminent massacre, they scratched their talons on the rocks to give them a keener edge. They licked their lips at the prospect of renting her flesh. Constantina was speechless as she watched her young Ullaunite companion walking to her certain death.

'Come back!' she implored.

At the sight of Boudicca's slow walk, the mob reacted with piteous grunting, shoulders jerking in simultaneous disdain. Boudicca in front of them closed her eyes and considered the blade out in the air. It was alone. A small wandering thing growing weaker, but doing its best to survive. She tapped into the weapon's heartbeat.

'Come to me. Come to my hand,' the phrase rolling around in her head. She repeated it. Boudicca opened her raised hand. Nothing happened. Constantina hung her head.

Unable to help themselves the Robusti launched toward her, from all sides. Then, from behind them, they heard the familiar whirring of Tarquin's blade, eagerly seeking its master.

'Boudicca!' Constantina shouted.

Boudicca jumped backward into the air, moving her hand at the wrist, grabbing the flying returner at the handle – too quick for her assailants. She cartwheeled backwards into the cave, millimetres out of reach of the pouncing mob.

Getting to her feet, Boudicca stood before Constantina with the returner in her hand and quickly gave it to Tarquin. Upon touching it he took a deep breath as if the weight of an anvil was lifted off his chest. Colour infused his face and raised veins smoothened. Constantina took a moment to consider exactly what her blind eyes had just witnessed.Constantina took a moment to consider exactly what her blind eyes had just witnessed.

'Who are you?' she bluntly asked, clicking furiously to gather more facts on events.

'You know who I am,' replied Boudicca.

'What I know does not bear out with what has just happened. So once again, who are you?'

'I'm Boudicca Moriarty. Granddaughter of Prospero and Nonie Moriarty, daughter of Sarah Moriarty. That is all I know.'

'Who is your father?'

Boudicca said nothing and shrugged her shoulders, before

bending down to help Tarquin to his feet and put his arm over her shoulder as they walked away. Constantina clicked to help navigate the cavernous darkness beyond. As they faded into that darkness, Jeybor looked on from a height and roared.

# Chapter 17

The Book of Mizar

*Chapter 4458*

*Verse 92*

*On learning the wind*

*It sweeps and comes round, and stops and what music it plays. That music stops with it and becomes defined by its absence; a silent music. The leaves are still and the branches no longer sway. Moving across the tops of corn, whispering Poseidon's song beneath. Some winds are born by stars, armed with a knowledge of the universe; some are born by gadfly's pinion. There is wisdom in both, as you breathe the wind, you breathe in the wisdom of many worlds.*

Every dark space of the forest was a potential ambush site.

Olor made his way through the woods, looking in all directions, always moving, never stopping, for stopping spelled the end. All the trees looked the same: colossal, titanic, gnarled with growth. Their gargantuan-sized and huge Jurassic leaves hung with the weight of their length. He had been running so long and fast that his steps were unsteady and slow. His legs were badly swollen.

The mob harried and pursued him, never once letting him rest or take refuge from the pursuit. He was the hunted and now almost caught. They could smell him, sniff his sweat off leaves and stalks that he had brushed or leaned against. His trail was obvious to their keen snouts. He was weak – and they knew it.

He found himself at a hillock on top of which sat flat rock. Around it, stood trees stripped of their branches and bark. The stench of ammonia was thick. The Robusti pissed here. He could hear them scream on all sides. His legs shook and gave way and he could run no longer. Olor now knew he had not stumbled here, but had been driven to this spot. With each passing moment, he came to terms with the finality of the circumstance. He was too tired and run down to do anything else. Would he cry out or remain silent, as each took their pound of flesh?

Olor's end-of-days notions were made real by Blacktooth landing in front of him with a fearful thud. He saw how much Blacktooth had grown, immensely so since the last time they had met, multiples of his previous size. Legs, arms and chest were swelled with brawn, veins bound his muscles, his knucklebones were balled and brutish. Blacktooth grabbed Olor by the throat and lifted him clean off the ground.

'Death has found you,' said Blacktooth, his eyes gleaming with a red tint.

Olor hung onto Blacktooth's wrist as blow after blow rained down on his face, splitting skin wherever they touched.

Blacktooth's fists pinged like hammers on anvils, battering Olor's head and flank, smashing against floating ribs and hips that were made of an inferior substance. He tried to shield his face from the blows. No grand ruse or escape plan came to mind, he was under enough pressure to stay conscious. All that kept him from slipping under was his force of will. A voice inside that said 'Hold on.' The mob gathered, excited and titillated by the certainty of the kill. They wondered whether Blacktooth would take his time or be overcome by the rush and kill the Grafter immediately.

'Who do you think you are? To deny me my kill,' said Blacktooth, playing to the crowd, Olor hanging from the nape of his neck. More blows, followed by headbutts. The mob howled with delight.

'To deprive me of my right – and deprive my cohort of the spectacle,' he continued.

A roar went up. Blood was desired, and Blacktooth was not going to disappoint. Olor wondered if there was enough blood in his body to satisfy them. Blacktooth and his cohort were in their element now – he gloried in their exaltation. They revelled in obedience to their new Lictor and the establishment of his order.

Blacktooth's roar shook the treetops and he tossed up Olor,

snatching him by the heel and dragging him to the flat rock in the middle of the hillock. Lying there, Olor barely breathed. His body possessed only the smallest traces of life. His eyes were open, yet swollen. Few could tell if he was still alive. Some were disappointed, thinking him already dead. He knew Blacktooth would mount the rock and devour him where he lay, starting with the eyes for delicacy then to the neck or chest. He would then call on the rest who would finish the job. Olor's bones would be stripped within seconds. The Grafter waited for the images of his life to float past his mind but nothing came.

Something else came instead. It was less of an image and more a sound, familiar and audible above the raucous din. The sound began to echo then turned into a far-off hooting. It was coming from the skies above. Through swollen eyes, Olor could just make out the shape of four swans, silhouettes making their way across the moon. He squinted as the birds descended and landed on a rock close by, waddling to a spot that overlooked the mob. Blacktooth took one more moment of adulation from his devotees. The Robusti began to shower him and Olor with spit, in ritual propitiation for execution.

As his shirt was ripped open for the kill, Olor heard a voice. It was cool and feminine, and came from the Swans.

*'Olor of the lake,*
*Soon to end your days of joy,*
*Soon to end your days of draíocht,*
*The darkness comes, 'til,*
*It is time to proclaim the dawn.'*

Olor felt his breath weaken and was sure that life would soon leave him. Blacktooth bent his knees and pounced onto the rock. Saliva was trickling from his gob, the sure sign of a deep appetite in his work. He placed his hand on Olor's neck, readying himself.

Everything fell silent. Time seemed to slow. Olor continued looking at the swans. From behind them, a hooded figure appeared, head bowed, face covered in shadow. With a slow movement, the figure pulled back the hood. Before him, stood the woman from the lake. His mother. Olor smiled at her.

Calmly she stared back. Her piercing blue eyes were filled

with pride and fury. He found peace in the depth of the moment. Olor never took his eyes off his mother. Slowly, she placed her hand across her chest, exposing the gold bracelet on her wrist. The moonlight bounced off it, catching Olor's weakening eyes. He looked at the identical bracelet in the palm of his own hand that now hung over the side of the rock slab.

'It is not your time,' said his mother. She raised her other hand, showing Olor two returners in her grip. The same returners Olor had seen on the boy at the lake.

Blacktooth raised his head and howled in anticipation of the execution. Opening his mouth, he descended upon Olor. As he did, two returners shot from the mother's hands landing in Olor's grip. In one movement and with energy from unknown sources, Olor plunged both returners into the temples of Blacktooth's still descending head. Plumes of blood gushed upward. The mob went apoplectic with exhilaration, spitting volumes and thinking themselves witness to a mighty execution. They were, but not the execution they coveted.

Blacktooth died instantly. He slumped on the slab of rock as his arms and legs gave way. His mouth was a hollow maw, his teeth no longer a threat, bared and grimacing in a deathly grin. It took a moment to push him off. But Olor did so, uprooting the returners in the process. The energy immediately drained away from the mob and was replaced by a panicked disorientation. Unsure of order and fearful of anarchy, they fled in chaotic directions.

Olor slowly and carefully picked himself up. With bloodied returners in each hand, he inhaled through his broken nose and swollen lips. The mob scampered off with barks and squeals, leaving their dead Lictor behind. Olor made his way to where the swans and his mother had been. All that remained were the sheaths and straps for his returners. Standing on the rock, he slowly tied the belt around his waist and hips. He slipped the gold bracelet onto his wrist, feeling its snug fit. As he was about to depart, the sound of a something moved behind him, making him reach for his returners. He turned to find a deer with antlers and a white stripe on his forehead. Olor knew it to be a Fia of the Ullaunites. The deer bowed. Another sign. Olor exhaled loudly and bowed in reply.

# Chapter 18

The Book of Alioth

*Chapter 2271*
*Verse 655*

*A badger awaits the rain to end at Rattle Pass*

*Sitting at the mouth of the sett.*

*The rain falls all over Rattle Pass.*

*Everything shines. Water rats brace the rushing river. I know none of their names now. I once knew their grandparents and those before them; but they have gone too. And so too will I. I hope this rain passes soon without taking the sett.*

The foul smell assailed their nostrils.

Inside the Chamber of Lloyb's cavernous bowels, Boudicca, Tarquin and Constantina navigated the darkness, unsure of their steps along a precarious ledge.

'It is their smell,' said Constantina, of the stench rising on warm air.

Tarquin moved forward, aided by a small light of the firefly dust on his fingertips. Behind him, Constantina enjoyed the confidence of someone now bestowed with sight while others were blind. Bringing up the rear was Boudicca, her smaller foot making her steps doubly unsure. The path was barely the width of a person and she was glad to be holding Constantina's hand.

'Stop!' whispered Constantina.

They halted, knowing Constantina's vision to be better than theirs.

'Continue,' she whispered, after sweeping the landscape with clicks.

'Do they eat Ullaunites?' asked Boudicca.

'They eat anything, supposedly,' said Tarquin.

'The Lloyb live in the cavities along these rocks. So, if you sense a hole, move away,' Constantina reminded them both.

They paused as Constantina clicked for their location and awaited coordinates.

'We will take this ridge to the end,' said Constantina. 'At places it is very narrow, so watch your step and keep your wits.'

'What lies beneath us?' enquired Boudicca.

'A river, home of the monstrous Gegoyn,' replied Constantina.

Over her clicks, they could hear the high-pitch squeals of the Gegoyn sloshing in the putrescent river below.

'Before Mustela began draining the Anam oil of Ullaunites, he drained it from animals. Some of the animals that survived became the Gegoyn,' she explained. She clicked again. 'At the end of this path, there is a rock. And on it is an altar.'

'What type of altar?' asked Tarquin.

'Sacrificial,' Constantina calmly replied.

'Charming,' said Tarquin, his eyes peering through the darkness.

'Beyond the altar, there is a passageway leading to the Tabernacle. It is a space they do not enter, for fear of the Pika. If we reach there, we will be safe.'

'The Pika?' said Tarquin.

'Their God,' Constantina replied. 'The one to whom they pray.'

Taking a breather, Tarquin placed his foot on a rock, which dislodged and rolled away. The result was a small avalanche of stones. The sound reverberated throughout the chamber. Nobody moved.

'Sorry.'

Constantina recalibrated their bearings once the echo of falling debris had diminished. As they moved on, she spotted a small hole in the wall – but too late. Suddenly, a swarm of Lloyb appeared, clinging to the rock face. Their toes were like fingers, fingers like toes.

In the darkened silence, their saucer eyes blinked as they let out a devilish call. 'PIKAAAAA! PIKAAAAA! PIKAAAAA!'

Three Lloyb landed on Constantina's shoulders. Another two

went to Tarquin. One brushed against Boudicca causing her to lose her footing. She fell from the ledge. Constantina tried to catch her – but she was gone, rolling toward the river below. Boudicca spun helplessly down the incline, hitting her head on a rock before landing in the thick soupy river.

'Run to the Tabernacle, Tarquin, run!' shouted Constantina, kicking and punching Lloyb attackers whenever she could.

'We can't leave her,' Tarquin called back.

'We will be taken if we stay. Go!' ordered Constantina.

Tarquin ran.

Sensing Constantina's isolation, the Lloyb reacted by converging on her, their menacing chant ringing out: 'Pika! Pika!' Constantina's clicks allowed her to see her attacker's bulbous eyes and the cracked skin of their hands and feet. Even though she sensed teeth, none bit her. With no time to unsheathe her returner, the Lloyb overpowered her quickly. They hoisted and carried her high as they moved forward to the cleft outcropping. She was needed alive: as a sacrifice. The Pika had to be pacified.

Ahead, Tarquin took more firefly dust from a pouch. Snapping his fingers as he went, energising the dust that lit his way toward safety. He couldn't see where Boudicca was, if she were alive or dead. Past the thin outcropping that Constantina had described, he finally reached the high Tabernacle. There, he found a flagstone behind which he spied a hole small enough to squeeze through. This is where he would position himself.

Focusing the firefly dust, like a powerful torch with a lens taken from his bag, he saw the massed throng make their way to their altar, with Constantina held above their heads. They emerged from their cloisters in their hundreds of thousands – possibly millions, the growing chant giving evidence of their mighty numbers. If he tried to save Constantina with returners, he was certain their numbers would overpower him.

Training the lens light on the river below, Tarquin could see Boudicca lying on the surface of the river, face up yet slowly sinking. What to do? Tarquin closed his eyes a moment. Logic and algebraic cadences jumbled in his deep thought; probabilities, arcs and tangents computed in his brain. A plan flashed like lightning in his mind. Many things would have to go his way, allied with good luck, but if his calculations were correct, he could save both Constantina and Boudicca.

The Lloyb procession brought Constantina to the altar, which stood wreathed with Robusti skulls and bones. Tarquin focused the light on one of the high priests. He was a little creature with no ears, and eyes that bulged from his face like pupilled bellies. His heart and lungs were visible through translucent skin. With a string of canines around his neck, he stood on the altar with his hands resting imperiously on small bony hips. The high priest delivered an acclamation to the Pika in a mixture of grunts, warbles and clicks that were unintelligible but received with animus and response by the congregation, who bowed and bobbed, humming gently in expectation. The Gegoyn emerged from their nests and positioned themselves to receive the scraps that would fall from the rocks above. Miraculously, they unknowingly swam past Boudicca.

Tarquin accessed the Pivot and through Ullaunite telepathy, he called on Constantina. 'Constantina! When you sense the light, run to the ivy vine. You hear? Run to the ivy.' He got no reply but sensed she had received the message. Tarquin got to work. He found another large rock, whispered his plan and complex algebraic computations into it, as if raising some sense within sharing his plan and then covered it with fire dust. He fastened one end of an ivy vine, taken from his bag, around the rock's middle. The other end, he attached to the flagstone at the Tabernacle's entrance. This mighty stone was to be an anchor point. Tarquin tossed the tethered rock as high as he could out into the cavernous space. As it fell, the dust lit up, ignited by the friction of the ivy rope. Tarquin could see massed ranks of Lloyb hanging from the walls and roof of the chamber.

The hefty rock continued its downward arc. Its ivy tether clung firmly to the rocky outcrop, the rock falling beneath, naturally creating a pendulum, the rock followed an arc and skimmed across the surface of the river. By Tarquin's calculations, there was just enough momentum in the swinging rock to complete the next two parts of his plan – but only if he was fast. First, he mind-triggered the blade of his returner, feeling an explosive energy entering the wooden grain, a white-hot light grew in the blade. Next, he seized another smaller fist-sized rock and covered it with fire dust. Quickly, he threw it into the air above the altar. He then launched his returner at it.

The Lloyb priest was now standing above Constantina's head, canines jingling as she strutted. He wielded an old Robustus jawbone as a knife and was about to complete the lethal covenant. Under many hands, Constantina, who had heard Tarquin's telepathy from the Pivot, calmed herself awaiting the signal. Tarquin's returner hit the mark, obliterating the rock into thousands of pieces. It set off a massive explosion of bright light that blinded the Lloyb's tender eyes. They cried out in pain, cowering from the shock of the brightness, shading their eyes beneath translucent arms and legs. Some fell from their perches. The Gegoyn below hungrily welcomed them to the river.

Constantina heard the explosion and felt the hands release her. It was now or never. Rising from the altar, she launched forward to the outcropping rock, clicking as she ran. Remnants of fire dust lingered in the air like dying fireworks on New Year's Eve. Tarquin could see the Lloyb regroup and give chase. Their sacrifice would not be given up easily. Constantina reached the edge and prepared to jump.

'Wait, Constantina, not yet,' shouted Tarquin, gauging the pendulum's swing. Constantina waited for what seemed like a million eternities. She heard the Lloyb almost upon her.

'Tarquin!'

'Now!' he roared.

Constantina leapt forward with as much power as she could muster. Some Lloyb followed her off the edge, limbs extended ready to grab. Their mouths were open, teeth baring. She could feel their bony fingers and toes grazing her just as the pendulous rock met her outstretched hand. She grabbed the ivy, the momentum pulling her away from her pursuers who plummeted into the gaping depths below.

Constantina swung over the filth and clicked to locate Boudicca. On the downswing she got a lock on her position. Constantina leaned out to grab her, but just missed, only dragging her fingertips across Boudicca's face, which had the effect of waking her. Tarquin saw that her movement and breathing was attracting the attention of the Gegoyn in the river and the banks.

'Tarquin!' Boudicca called out, in terror.

Constantina reached him on the apex of her upward swing. By his calculations, she only had one attempt left to get Boudicca and her back to safety.

'Make this count,' he said, bluntly.

Constantina understood and nodded. She then turned herself upside-down to swing, head-first. On her downswing, she pulled her two returners from their sheaths on her back and spun them skilfully in her hands. Constantina could see that the Gegoyn had now surrounded Boudicca. They were sizing her up, brushing against one another as if arguing over who would have first dibs on the Ullaunite. Throughout all this, Boudicca kept her hand raised.

'I see you, Boudicca!' Constantina called – locked and loaded.

Just then, a Gegoyn rose from the filth. Eyeless and scaly, teeth in clusters like raspberries on the bramble, it turned in the air, its mouth gaping, about to gobble up Boudicca. As it breached, Constantina despatched a returner and sliced off the top of its head. Another Gegoyn attempted a similar attack. The second returner did a similar job. In the sloshing throes of the dying behemoths, Boudicca found herself being dragged deeper into the filth. As she sank up to her eyes and nostrils, Constantina lost signal with Boudicca's hand.

'Raise your hand,' she shouted. Swing, and a miss. Constantina clicked furiously. This was it: her next descent would be her final chance. It would need precision. But right now, she could not lock on Boudicca's position. The disturbance on the filth had subsumed her.

Tarquin's algebra skills were being similarly scrambled. His calculations had factored in the weight of two bodies on the vine but not the energy of the swing required for one body to pull another from the suction of the filth. His Ullaunite arithmetic did not stack up. Even if Boudicca did emerge, they would be too heavy to complete the final swing together. He was horrified. 'Come on Boudicca. Give me a sign.'

On what would be the final descent, Constantina clicked furiously. She could sense the Gegoyn moving just below the filth, all-making their way to one convergent spot. 'A hand Boudicca,' thought Constantina, opening her mind to Boudicca through the Pivot.

The murky water below turned calmer. Constantina clicked, looking for signs of anything as she swung. She could again sense movement. The Gegoyn continued to converge on one spot. Holding onto the rock, she repositioned herself to get maximum velocity. She saw something small move in the filth. Constantina locked on and pushed off. On the last moments of her final approach, it rose from the filth. A hand. She hoped Boudicca was attached below the wrist. Constantina grabbed it.

Boudicca emerged from the depths, with a Gegoyn rising in hungry pursuit, its open jaws snapping down on what was now thin air and landing with a splash as its prey escaped. Constantina used all her strength to hang onto the young Ullaunite. As Tarquin feared, the mathematics began to fail as the pair struggled to reach the apex of the swing. At the last moment, Constantina threw Boudicca to Tarquin, who caught her and dragged her to safety. Constantina swung away.

'Are you alright?' asked Tarquin.

Boudicca coughed and nodded.

Without the velocity to reach the top of the arc, Constantina realised that only one choice remained. The only way was down, she thought. At the point of optimal elevation, she would jump for her life. She readied herself as she swung away. Her hair and clothing fluttered in the passing air. She reached the point where the rock stopped at its greatest height and she returned, standing on the rock and with dying velocity, one last time. At the highest point of the upswing, still a distance away from her compatriots, Constantina jumped.

Boudicca looked on, time felt as if it had slowed. It was like nothing she had ever seen. The beauty of Constantina's movement in the air. Somersaulting, feet pointed; body twisting and turning; gaining maximum height, air and momentum. Boudicca saw her open her palms and from the darkness, her returners, that had been despatched earlier, landed in her snug grip. And then she fell from view.

The only sound in the darkness was a splash in the filth below added to by the sound of the Gegoyn, busy in their screaming and frenzy.

'It can't be,' whispered Tarquin.

Boudicca's heart sank. Both were certain that Constantina Pipistrelle was lost. They looked dumbstruck trying to comprehend their monumental loss. Their hearts thumped with shock and then grew weak with reality. Dumb wide eyes said everything and nothing. The splashing died away, the screams of the Gegoyn muffled under the levels below.

Tick. Tick. Tick. Tick. Boudicca heard it first. Tick. Tick. Tick. Tick. There it was again, a slight sound coming from below. Tarquin thought it sounded like sheoak piercing rock. Surely … not? As they peered over the edge of the precipice, they could see nothing. A trick of the imagination perhaps. Then came a clicking sound. Constantina! It was her, using her returners to dig into the rock and climb toward the ledge of the Tabernacle. They helped her as best they could, pulling her over the ledge until they all collapsed with exhaustion.

After catching her breath, Constantina broke the silence. 'Good plan, Tarquin. It worked.'

'Algebra is nothing without bravery,' he replied, in equal parts relief and awe.

Boudicca wiped her face with her filthy hand, making her face even filthier.

'You saved my life,' said Boudicca. 'Thank you.'

'We are all alive – and that's all that matters,' said Constantina.

Without another word, they crawled through the Tabernacle entrance and onward to the middle chamber of Mount Bolcawn.

# Chapter 19

The Book of Alioth

*Chapter 60*
*Verse 8561*

*A cob sits while his pen feeds*

*She feeds in silence while I nest. Seven beneath her and we pray to the Bradán that all will see light. Pen thinks the last turn of the second moon will bring them forth.*

*She knows these things. She knows more than me.*

The sound of pistons echoed through the heart of Mount Bolcawn.

Their driving surge processing Anam oil as they sucked and pushed the golden elixir through pipes and valves then churned and spun it through filters and chambers. The clinical industrial science that Mustela had brought to the Ullauns underpinned his strength and the rise of the Regnum.

The Ullaunites being processed lay silently suspended in their vats. They were held in what was a perfect state of the extraction. A dull hinterland of consciousness located between the second last and last breath of life, a featureless borderland rich with oil and little else. The longer they stayed barely alive, the more they produced an oil which the Regnum craved.

Fabul and Berl were the on-duty Lictors rostered this day. 'Divide et Impera' they saluted, crossing one other along a gangway above the vats. They walked with a leggy nonchalance, heels touching the floor well before the balls of their feet, delighting in the deliciousness of the power bestowed on them. Unexpectedly, these serf-kings were interrupted by a more mundane sound: a bell that signalled a problem in one of the lines.

Teams sprang into action, setting about their individual tasks. Tubing was checked. Valves were examined. Possibilities were excluded. Eventually, the lackey hoards located the offending vessel, finding the errant specimen amongst the thousands in stasis.

'U4703,' came the call.

The number repeated from one to the other, like a whispered secret. Lists were checked, fingers trapezing across pages and then down columns.

'Giorra.'

U4703 was Finn Giorra's vessel.

Robusti gathered around the vat, peering through the glass into the fluid. Berl saw the piping attached to Finn's heart had moved from his chest cavity and was now floating in the fluid. Small trickles of blood rising from its steely tip and the hole vacated. The vessel would need to be emptied quickly and the specimen taken from the tank. Otherwise, this prized Ullaunite would drown – a disaster. Mustela's wrath would be brutal if the Ullanite was lost.

On Berl's command Robusti operatives moved to their posts, readying themselves for the emergency procedure. Step one required pulling a sinkhole lever to drain the vat of preserving fluid. Two Robusti operatives fought over the right to pull the lever, quickly agreeing to pull it together in a surprising entente cordiale. They did so, smiling with idiotic pride. Nothing happened. They returned the lever to its original position and pulled again, expecting a different result. Still nothing.

'Stop!' roared Berl, over the still ringing alarm bell.

'Ullaunite drown,' said Fabul.

'Must save oil,' replied Berl.

Fabul nodded and turned to his cohort.

They looked at one another tensely. This needed "Emergency Procedure Step Two."

'Axe!' shouted Fabul.

'Axe. Axe. Axe.' The word echoed through the chamber. Operatives headed off in clueless directions search of "Axe". One returned proudly, presenting it to Fabul with a reverential whisper: 'Axe'

Fabul handed it to Berl.

'You do,' he said.

Berl took the axe, leaned back and struck the glass surface with all his strength. The axe bounced out of his hand and hit an on-looking Robustus – cleaving his forehead and killing him instantly.

'Oops,' said Berl.

None cared for the dead Robustus.

'Again,' Fabul called.

Berl was about to strike when he saw the birth of a crack growing around the glass. Slowly, it branched out, jagged and untamed. The group stood back in awe as they watched it spread further and further.

The weight and pressure of the fluid smashed the glass, inundating the floor and sending Robusti reeling from the force. When the wave subsided, they peered through the broken glass of the chamber and couldn't see Finn Giorra in the vat.

'Where be, Giorra?'

'Where he be?' asked Berl, looking around.

'Where he be?' parroted a confused Fabul.

They both shouted looking around on the floor.

'Where he be?'

From behind, they heard a sound of throat clearing.

They all turned

'He be here.' A stony-faced Finn Giorra replied, '… and he be thirsty for revenge.'

Finn stood there drenched and partially naked. Blood trickled from his chest, past his bellybutton. More trickled from his forehead. He leaned back and opened his jaws. Fabul and Berl watched wide-eyed as Finn reached deep into his own throat and regurgitated a sheoak blade, he had earlier secreted there. Pulling it up from his gut. He then released a clasp on the blade point; splitting it down its long edge to create two returners. Finn eyed his enemies and presented arms with a flourish, and like the hare that he was, thumped his foot twice on the floor. The Robusti responded with the confidence of numbers. It did not save them.

When it was all over, Finn stood panting, his blades still quivering. His skin was spattered with blood. Robusti bodies lay at his feet. He needed to act fast. He ran to the glass vessel containing his sister, climbing the plinth as quickly as he could, his legs shaking with every step. Hearing the grunts of another cohort closing in, he knew he had to be quick.

He removed a tooth from his mouth – a molar crowned with a diamond. "Good man, Old Joe as clever an Ullaunite as ever was,' said Finn to himself. Placing the diamond on the tank, he drew a circle on the glass with the diamond and intersected it with two lines. He kissed the tooth in thanks and put it back into his mouth. He leaned down and collected the axe used on his vat. His weak arms shook as he lifted it. He was still seeping blood from his heart and head. He struck the vat on the cross-section of the circle. The axe bounced. It sent a shock up the shaft and painfully into his hands. Over his shoulder, he could see Robusti – much greater numbers than before – launching themselves forward, running on knuckle and ball.

He turned and saw the vessel crack, like a taproot it began to spread, metastasizing around the curve of the glass. 'Come on,' he said, coaxing the crack to greater ambition. The glass shattered and collapsed, sending liquid in the direction of the approaching group, halting their front-runners and sending the rest crashing into them from behind.

Finn reclaimed Ashket, keeping her steady while de-needling her. She lay slumped in his arms, but he took great comfort in holding his sister once more, even though she was barely alive. Lifting her over his shoulder, she felt lighter than before. An effect of muscular atrophy, a direct result of her stasis. He could sense her Anam was low and her body in shock.

'Ashket, this is Finn. You have to stay alive, for as long as you can. You hear, for as long as you can,' he pleaded. He reached for his returners on the ground. The two blades reformed as one and jumped into his hand. Inching around the back of the vats, he climbed one of the stairwells leading to the gangways above. They were attached to the roof by stanchions and ropes.

The Robusti saw him move. They felt confident that he could be run down, now that he was carrying the extra weight. Finn's weakened gait excited the mob even more. They split into two groups, one joining Finn and Ashket on the gangway, the other following below.

Finn's breathing was also laboured as his Anam was already depleted. Ahead, he saw a segment of the gangway hanging from a point of intersection. Running through the intersection, Finn despatched his returner toward the holding point. With sparks flying, it sliced through the holding chain. It gave way easily. Forty Robusti, who had run unwittingly onto the gangway, crashed down upon the chasing group below. The rest poured over their trapped comrades, uncaring and unwavering in the need to capture the Ullaunites.

Finn's returner landed in his hand. Without breaking stride, he jumped down to ground level and toward a corridor of vats, leading to a door ahead. It was locked.

Much weakened now, he tried to open the door with whatever reserves of Anam he had left. The door handle turned, but the inner mechanisms of the lock had rusted and seized. It would not open.

Finn turned to find their hunters within striking distance. The pair were trapped. The giggling mob morphed into a growling one. Robusti crowded in on the pair. Finn and Ashket were now pinned in with their backs to the rock wall. Finn's pinhole wounds wept. He could hear his chest-hole whistle with every breath. He backed into the corner and stood, with Ashket on his shoulder. The Robusti knew the dance of the trapped. Taking it in turns, some would attack from the left, others from the right. Soon Finn would grow tired and let them take their prize. They knew how the dance would end: he would be overpowered and that would be that.

'I am sorry sister, this is as far as we go it seems,' said Finn, gathering her close. Ashket opened her eyes.

'Take as many as you can. Somnia Sine Metu,' she ordered, with her last ounce of life she could muster.

Finn's eyes welled with pride. He kissed his sister on the cheek, and faced the mob with his returner raised.

Finn had no sooner turned, when he heard a low rumbling sound coming from deep within the walls behind them. A sound that was accompanied by searing heat. At his back, plumes of smoke seeped through the walls. The ore within the rock seemed to melt and drip as the wall parted like molten curtains being

drawn open. In the hollowed-out cavity, Finn counted six returners hovering in the air, and could see figures emerging through
the smoke. The Robusti reared up onto their hinds and retreated
a few steps, apprehensive at the sight of the destruction and the
appearance the new arrivals.

'Am I glad to see you!' said Finn.

Boudicca, Constantina and Tarquin stood before him.

'How did you know where we'd be?'

'Our returners led us,' said Constanina. 'They sensed yours.'

'All will hear of your deeds, this day,' added Tarquin.

They all smiled and moved forward.

'Boudicca, can you take care of Ashket and Finn for a moment?'
asked Constantina. 'We have bloody business to attend.'

Boudicca nodded.

Tarquin and Constantina regathered their returners and strode
toward the Robusti with deadly purpose.

# Chapter 20

The Book of Dubhe

*Chapter 1220*
*Verse 90213*

*On a blackbird's silence*

*I am in the seventh moon and the dying night has brought with it*
*a Boreal from the northern waters. The great star is rising.*
*I have fallen from my perch and am too weak to regain it.*
*I dare not sing for there is a stoat about, a stoat about.*
*It is so cold. I must remain silent. There is a stoat about, a stoat*
*about. But then again, here comes the great star.*
*I must sing … I must sing.*

The room was quiet. Not silent, but as close as possible to silence. For there is always sound, even underground.

Ithaca sat on the edge of his bed, hands moving over his armlets. The tips of his fingers drew softly across the designs on his leathers, the buckles on his waistcoat, the returners on his hips. He clicked his tongue, sensing the empty space. He could sense the outline and form of the room, the plain state of things like borders and shapes, but nothing else. No colours. No textures. He put his hands on the bed and felt the warmth left by his hand on the softness of the blanket, and how the warmth was held for a moment, then lost by the careless wool. He concentrated on the phenomenology of the tactile, not wishing to let his mind slip into Fate's endless spin of possibilities and improbabilities.

Not having his sister near was a wrench. Something that left him feeling cold. It was as if Death was near, but not yet interested in him, only in those whom he loved, preserving its sting for someone else. If his sister did not return, he thought, this cold emptiness was something he would have to live with for the rest of his days. Blindness would make it doubly hard, but he would bear it privately, and in silence. And yet, his blind eyes began to well up. Ithaca put his hand on his returner and heard his heart thump in his chest.

Just then, there was a knock at the door.

'Yes?' called Ithaca, composing himself with a sniffle.

'It is me – Old Joe,' said a croaking voice, from outside.

Ithaca opened the door. He clicked, quickly getting a sense of the person. They hadn't talked since The Sopor, and the figure that entered was a different being; hunched over, joints swollen, fluid gathering on all parts. Ithaca could scarcely believe the old man's state.

'Ithaca,' said Old Joe, wheezing. 'A word, if you will.'

'Please, sit.' Ithaca helped him into a chair.

'I'm not feeling well, child'

'Will I fetch Liam Sciurus, to rustle up a brew from his herbs?' asked Ithaca.

Old Joe coughed, a brief smile passing over his face. 'There is very little that grows that can cure grief and shame.' He blinked and paused. 'I have come to thank you for what you did. This is a time of great importance, where futures lie in the balance. Having seen many of my kind go before me, I wish to thank you for this opportunity.'

'What opportunity?' asked Ithaca, puzzled.

'To cast off the trappings of being, and thus becoming truly at one with the Ullauns. 'Here. Take this, a form of thanks.' Old Joe passed him a muslin pouch.

'What is it?'

'A new invention of mine.'

Ithaca opened the pouch and took out a ring. In it sat two blue sapphires. Joe looked down and saw the light flashing through them.

'Recut sapphires, from the mines of Riyerk. It was a present for my wife that I never had a chance to give to her.'

'Ryerk. I thought that a place of myth,' said a disbelieving Ithaca.

'What we don't understand takes the form of myth,' replied

Joe, smiling.

'This is too precious, I can't,' Ithaca protested.

'Shhh, I'm not finished,' Old Joe, curtly 'My father was blind too, you know. Clicked like you ....'

'Blind,' Ithaca interrupted, looking up from the rings, still feeling them with his thumbs and forefinger.

'Yes, blind,' continued Old Joe. 'Now listen. I have been working on this for many moons – in secret – with the help of some star-nosed moles. It is not the problem solved, but it might be something of interest to you.'

Ithaca clicked at the ring and then to the old man.

'Put it on. The ring ... put it on,' Old Joe wheezed.

Ithaca could hear a smile in his voice. Slowly and with care, Ithaca slipped it on his finger. Nothing happened.

'There might be a little pain at first, but stay with it,' Old Joe cautioned.

It took a few seconds. Ithaca gave a perceptible wince as a jolt of pain erupted at the back of the temples, behind his eyes. He placed his hand on the bridge of his nose and breathed. Then opening his eyes, he looked around.

'Well?'

Ithaca was dumbstruck. For the first time in his life, he was assailed by the sensation of colour. He could see that the stones on the ring were an iridescent blue. He could see the light of his candle on the table. Not full sight but definitely more than he had experienced in the past. Tears erupted from his eyes: he could now see colour. It was a sensorial swell that he hadn't prepared for; couldn't prepare for. Silence seemed to be the most appropriate way to come to terms with the experience.

'Thank you, Joe,' said Ithaca, after a pause. He daren't say more.

'It is I who must thank you,' replied Old Joe.

Ithaca could feel something else in the pouch. He took out another ring with the similar stones on it.

'For your sister when she returns,' said Joe, turning to Ithaca.

Joe then closed his eyes.

'Joe?' called Ithaca. There was no movement, Joe was unresponsive. Ithaca knelt down beside him. 'Joe Martes, can you hear me?' He looked to the door and opened it. 'Liam!' he cried. 'Liam Sciurus, Old Joe has taken ill. Old Joe has taken ill.'

# Chapter 21

The Book of Mizar

*Chapter 45*
*Verse2*

*A summer gale ponders its origin*

*I started in the first moon and it is now the fourth. A young star-ling on the edge of his nest, gave a flutter, and it was there I began.*
*I joined others and others joined us and I moved from the land out to sea.*
*Now I return as a gale, howling my shanty. Beware my shanty for it will make landfall soon and your trees and your corn will dance.*

Near the vats in the belly of Mount Bolcawn, the returners ceased and were calm.

Finn turned to Ashket, delighted to see colour return to her face. Both now were dressed in muslin shirts and pants provided by Tarquin from his backpack.

'You came for me,' Ashket said, to her brother.

'We all did. You would have done the same for us,' replied Finn, hugging her closely.

They all took a moment to bask in their happy reunion. But as reality dawned on how trapped they really were, thoughts quickly turned to escape.

'Have you considered a way out?' asked Finn.

Both Constantina and Tarquin shook their heads glumly. They hadn't really bargained on getting this far.

'We could go back the way we came,' said Tarquin.

'Without the element of surprise, that is impenetrable,' Constantina replied, flatly.

While they silently considered their options, nobody was taking much notice of Boudicca. She was looking at the contents of the vats, emotionless, gathering her thoughts.

Eventually Finn walked to her. 'Mustela will pay for this,' he affirmed, taking a moment to cast his eye over the vats. Boudicca looked straight ahead at nothing in particular.

'What would we need to get out alive?' she asked, as if lost in thought.

'A miracle,' answered Finn.

'Think deeply again and answer the question. What would we need to get out alive?' asked Boudicca.

Finn was taken aback by the intensity of this newly arrived Ullaunite's questioning. 'I don't know,' said Finn. 'An army?'

'What about a sleeping army,' said Boudicca, looking into his eyes. The moment seemed to expand, their eyes not moving. A comfort lay there, accompanied by a rush.

'An army,' said Finn, with a smile. The realisation dawned on him.

Boudicca turned without saying a word and walked to the locked door. 'I think the oil is here,' she announced. She tried to open it, but was unsuccessful. It wouldn't budge. She tried a running kick with her good foot, but her smaller foot gave way beneath her.

'Let me,' offered Constantina, who aimed her foot and powerfully kicked the door off its hinges.

Inside was more vast than the previous chamber. They found innumerable enormous glass vats. They reckoned twenty times the size of the ones containing the Ullaunites. All of them connected and bubbling with amber fluid. Finn, Tarquin, Ashket and Boudicca walked around slowly surveying them, sniffing the thick scent of Anam in the air, tapping them with their returners. They could barely fathom the industrial immensity of what was being done here.

'To have an army we must return this oil to their owners,' declared Boudicca.

'Tarquin? How long do you think it would take?' asked Finn.

'Weeks … months, maybe,' replied Tarquin.

'We don't have that.'

'We must signal the others back at Cumann Rock,' said Tarquin.

'How?' asked Constantina.

Finn looked at the hole from which the others had emerged.

'We must dig with our returners,' said Tarquin.

'Of course,' said Constantina.

'I can let off the rest of my fire dust from outside. They will surely see that. I will need help though,' said Tarquin, seeing a plan take shape.

'I can help too,' said Ashket'

'Rest, Ashket,' said Finn. 'Let us find your returner first.'

'The others will join you soon,' said Boudicca, to the group, as she began to climb a ladder attached to the side of a vat leading to the rim at the top.

'What others?' asked Tarquin.

Boudicca didn't reply.

'Where are you going, Boudicca?' Constantina called after her.

Boudicca was getting more anxious the higher she climbed. With each step she found it harder to breath. The group looked on uneasily.

'Tarquin, Constantina, Finn,' said Boudicca. 'We are braver when we're together. Your job is to save the Ullauns, mine is to find my mother.' With that Boudicca jumped feet first into the vat and was swallowed by the oil.

The others looked on in astonishment, not believing what they just witnessed. They raced to the vat and looked frantically inside but couldn't see her in the murkiness. Nothing happened for a moment. Finn then pointed to a low level of light glowing within the depths. It began to grow in intensity, moving from vat to vat through interconnecting pipes. They all saw the light grow from the vats and then move along the pipes into the next room back to the vats containing the Ullaunites. Ashket, who had been weak 'til that moment – found immediate strength and got to her feet.

The background hum of the pumps and pistons ceased. Quietness reigned and the Ullanites looked to each other. Slowly, the vats began to drain of their oil. The Anam oil was beginning to flow in the opposite direction, back to the Ullaunites from which it came.

'I need my returner, Finn,' Ashket demanded.

'If you're strong enough, then get it,' said Finn, with mild excitement.

She closed her eyes. All the captured Ullaunite weapons were in a nearby cavern. Mustela knew the power of having them close by and they sat in a giant heap at the hairy feet of snoozing Robusti guards. Ashket's lay on top of the pile. Now having enough strength to locate it, she reached out her hand to call it back. The returner rattled – loud enough for the sleeping guard to wriggle his nose and open one eye. Conscious of being watched, it waited until the Robusti's eyes closed again, then pulled itself clear of the pile. Hovering silently for a moment, it slipped beneath the door, and sped with anticipation and joy to return to its owner. Without making a sound, the weapon flew down passageways, passed through cavern doors and climbed to the shadows above the heads of oblivious Robusti. Sensing Ashket close by, it gained speed like a lost child returning to its mother. Then, it stopped abruptly … one-eighth of an inch from her hand. Ashket opened her eyes and slowly wrapped her fingers round the hilt. A white glow radiated from the blade. Reunited with her weapon, life immediately surged though her body, re-energising her strength.

'Do you hear that?' asked Constantina.

Everyone listened.

'It's the sound of a thousand returners waking,' she said.

Everyone knew Boudicca had done this.

Soon the air was filled with the sound of smashing glass vats and the whirr of returners landing in the open palms of the captive Ullaunites. With their Anam and strength returned they each began to unpipe their heads and hearts. Minute by minute, an army of thousands was being awakened from their torpor, ready to fight. Soon, the great vats were empty and the Ullaunites who slept there had now awoken, knowing of their loss and yet grateful they had survived their fate. They had a chance to redeem themselves; to fight the Regnum again; to dream without fear again. Weakened, but ready with their returners in their hands, they bowed to those who had released them.

Many stayed and fought the Robusti where they stood. Others, on command, joined Ashket and Tarquin using their returners to dig up through the mountain, to the starry sky outside. Before long the group emerged from the side of the mountain, unnoticed by the Robustopolis below. Cutting a channel in a rock he picked up from the ground, Tarquin tied to it the pouch containing the remainder of his firefly dust. Throwing it high into the air, Ashket released her returner to pursue it. When they met, the explosion lit the mountain and the surrounds like it was a summer noon. The signal had been given.

Finn climbed up the side of the vat and stood on the rim. Below him, he could see Boudicca lying at the bottom of the vessel empty of its oil.

'She's there,' Finn called out.

Constantina cut open the base of the vat with her returner. They found Boudicca covered in oil but they could see her chest moving. She was breathing but in a deep sleep.

'She's alive,' said Constantina, carrying Boudicca to safety on her shoulders.

'Who is this Ullaunite?' Finn asked in wonderment.

Constantina looked at the others and smiled.

'She says she's just, Boudicca Moriarty ... but I suspect she is something else entirely.'

# Chapter 22

The Book of Alkaid

*Chapter 976*
*Verse unnumbered*

*A leveret hangs in a barn owl's talons*

*What knowledge is this?*
*I see it all now. The fields; I see where they lie and beyond are the*
*mountains. I heard of them, but never saw them.*
*A farmyard nearby, we circle above it, to the side of the yard is an*
*orchard, that my father convinced me was a myth. I see the apples*
*and they are heavy and red and delicious to the eye. We now circle*
*above a field of near ripe corn; the owls talons are soft on my skin.*
*We enter a barn. Ahead I see three wide-eyed hungry chicks.*
*What knowledge is this?*
*A knowledge of my end.*

The glasses clinked in her hands. Niamh held the small medical
bottles close to her chest, careful not to drop any. Their contents
were written on white labels in Liam's clear hand, a collection of
natural ingredients requested by him in emergency to save Joe's
life. Ground Elder, Borage, Tansy, Sage, Shaggy Ink Cap, Penny
Bun, Fly Agaric. She placed them on the table while he worked
with pace on the pestle and mortar.

Old Joe lay in the bed, his face blanched and grey, mouth open,
coughing often. With each breath he grew weaker and his life
force diluted away.

'What's the matter with him?' asked Ithaca.

'Shame,' replied Liam.

Ithaca and Gannymeade stood at the end of his bed, unsure of
the precise state of Old Joe's health. All they knew was it looked

like he was getting worse, and close to the end. On the other side of the bed was Tycho, holding a damp cloth and occasionally dabbing Joe's forehead. The old man looked cold as if death had crept into the bed beside him. However, Tycho felt intense heat coming from his skin.

Liam worked quickly, adding the ingredients Niamh had gathered. Outside Alba stood sentry, keeping watch for a sign from Mount Bolcawn.

'What is it Liam?' asked Gannymeade.

'His grief has become infected by the shame he feels for his mistakes,' he said, not lifting his head from his grinding. 'I can see the work of the Scawl here, and every atom of Joe is fighting the infection. Though the fight weakens him.'

'Is there anything we can do?' asked Tycho.

'Nothing Tycho,' said Liam. 'The question is what can I do?'

'Which is …?'

'Administer this – and hope for the best.'

Everyone was a little shocked at Liam's directness of speech.

Niamh noticed them appraising her brother and immediately felt protective of him. 'Liam can be very focused,' she said, in an almost apologetic way.

Liam took out his returner. He then used a small spoon, scooping up some of the ground dust in the mortar and tapping it out on the end of his blade, which began to glow and grow hot. The dust began to let off a heavy smoke. He asked Niamh quickly to hand him the open jar, which she did. Liam turned it upside down to gather as much of the smoke as possible. He tapped the returner on the edge of the table and put it back in its scabbard.

He turned to Tycho. 'Place both your hands over Joe's mouth and nose, form a beehive shape there, leaving an opening on top for the jar.'

Tycho did as requested.

Liam placed the jar on the opening. They all saw Old Joe inhale the smoke after which he began to settle in the bed. Almost immediately, his breathing became regular, colour returning to his face, smoke rolling out of his nostrils like searching roots.

'Well done,' said Tycho, relief visible in his eyes.

'It is just a relaxant. The battle rages still,' said Liam. 'He must fight the infection. I can do no more, he must heal himself.'

Momentarily Old Joe opened his eyes. Tycho saw this and clutched his hand.

'Help my boy, Tycho,' said Old Joe. 'If I die, then the Boreals will take me.'

Tycho nodded. 'I'll see you soon, Joe?'

'I hope so,' the old man replied.

Alba Sciurus called from outside. They all responded and found her standing on a rock, with her returner out of its sheath. Boudicca's Fia stood beside her, his massive antlers proud on his head. On his back, sat a beaten and bloodied Olor.

Every Ullaunite drew their weapon on sight of their sworn enemy. Except Gannymeade, who walked towards him and slowly offered her hand. He took it and slumped into her embrace from the deer's back. She held him up as he steadied himself on his feet. He trembled in her arms.

'Olor.'

'Gannymeade,' he replied, bowing deferentially.

Alba moved forward defiantly.

'Look at his returners, Alba,' said Gannymeade.

'He's … Ullaunite?' asked a baffled Alba.

'Yes,' replied Gannymeade. 'Always was, and always will be.'

Olor looked up and thanked her with his eyes.

Gannymeade nodded and turned her head to the healer. 'Liam Sciurus, can you physic him?'

'His returners will,' said Liam, stepping closer to assess Olor's injuries in greater detail.

'Who did this?'

'Blacktooth,' replied Olor.

'And what of him?'

'He is no more.'

'Good work. Now, unsheath your returners,' instructed Liam.

He did as requested, 'Touch the blade ends together and repeat after me, *'Ullaunite, cura te ipsum'*.

Olor repeated the incantation. Immediately, the blood ceased to flow from his wounds and they began to heal. The swelling in his eyes began to decrease as if punctured, the blisters on his hand disappeared. Within seconds, there were only a few scratches on his face, weeks of healing realised in a moment.

'Thank you,' whispered Olor.

Liam nodded and shook his hand.

'Are you alone?' asked Gannymeade.

'Others have followed the Fia,' said Olor, looking down from the prow of the hill.

They followed his gaze and were greeted by the sight of thousands of deer arranged in formation – all with their antlers bright and pointed, heads bobbing, and readying themselves for an engagement.

'It was the Fia, not I,' admitted Olor.

Gannymeade smiled and bowed toward the mass ranks of deer. They replied in kind.

'If we survive this day, we will hear of Olor and his Ullaunite provenance,' proclaimed Gannymeade, to the group.

Just then a light flashed from above Mount Bolcawn in a huge explosion. It lit up their faces and all eyes squinted at the diurnal brightness that hung in the air like a mighty midnight sun. Quickly, the edges began to die away, revealing a glitter. It was the trail of firefly dust – and they all knew it to be the signal.

'Gannymeade,' called a voice, from behind.

Gannymeade looked around and saw Old Joe standing at the door of Cumann Rock. The colour had returned to his face though he was still hunched over.

'That is him. That is my boy,' he said with a smile. 'Bring him home.'

'We will. Return to your bed and better yourself,' said Tycho.

Old Joe nodded and went inside with a smile.

Gannymeade ordered the Fia into divisions lead by an Ullaunite. She directed them to split off toward different parts of the Ullauns and to attack the mountain from every side. 'Somnia Sine Metu,' she called out.

'Somnia Sine Metu,' replied the group, raising their returners. The Fia roared.

# Chapter 23

The Book of Megrez

*Chapter 8*
*Verse8*

*A caterpillar considers a new leaf*

*There is another juicy leaf.*
*Such gorging before magic,*
*I know what lies ahead see. It is in me. I dream as I eat. The dream*
*requires energy, it grows as I gorge. How big will my wings be?*
*Ah haaa,*
*As the dream grows, I grow. I am in the dream now.*

They slowed down, knowing they were in dangerous territory.

Finn had run ahead with his returners unsheathed. Constantina carried a drowsy Boudicca on her shoulders. They had been running through a network of tunnels. Before they knew it, they stepped into a large dark cavernous space. Their echoed footsteps alerted them to the size of the space.

'Constantina, what do you see?' asked Finn, when they regrouped.

A whispered voice came from the darkness. 'Do not rely on the blind for sight.' It was Mustela.

A flame caught light and grew quickly through the channels on the walls of the cavern. They were in Mustela's chamber and he stood in the middle on his island of weasels, which did not move or squeal, as if dormant.

'You are persistent little things,' Mustela hissed. 'Like a gadfly in summer. But, like them, you too will be swotted away.'

His Praetorian, Decima, stepped out ominously from behind him.

'Where are my manners …? Have you met Decima?'

Decima disrobed from her cloak and cowl with a roll of her impressive shoulders. Spartan armour covered her chest, shoulders, flanks, and groin. Each muscle on her form seemed hewn from rock and massive in their size. The bones of her face protruded, as if dislocated, beneath skin of cold alabaster. Her ears were big, and pinched out from the side of her head. A cat-o'-nine-tails hung on her hip. With an exaggerated flourish, she produced a scimitar from a scabbard. The Ullaunites backed themselves against the wall. Constantina placed the still sleeping Boudicca gently on the ground. They presented their returners as a prelude to engagement.

'A pleasure to fight with you,' said Finn, turning to Constantina.

'Likewise,' replied Constantina.

They sprang forward and engaged the Praetorian.

Decima proved herself to be strong and elusive, landing heavy blows on the Ullaunites. Finn and Constantina fought at a frenetic pace with speed and skill, as was their way. But the force of Decima's repeated blows began to take their toll. Severely weakened, the Ullaunite pair's fight ended with both being hurled with such force that they raised a cloud of dust as they landed in a heap on the floor. They lay unconscious beside Boudicca.

Decima turned to Mustela and bowed, who weakly applauded her engagement. In his own time he announced with a hint of disappointment, 'All that is left of the once-great Ullaunite nation. Such majesty!' He moved forward menacingly on a dais of weasels. 'I took on the might of this nation, a tribe fat with injustice. They scorned me. Branded me. Expelled me. And now all that remains is this band of reprobates, withering and starved, the wretched of the Ullauns.' He paused, letting the silence wreathing his words. 'I control all now.'

A messenger Lictor appeared at the doorway.

'What?' barked Mustela, taking umbrage at the unwelcome intrusion.

'There is an attack on two fronts, sire. The first is from within: Ullaunites have been raised from the vats and have escaped, armed with their returners.'

Mustela seethed at the news. His weasels raised a deafening squeal.

'And the second?' Mustela asked vacantly.

'Gannymeade, and her remaining forces attack the Mountain mounted on …'

'On what?' said Mustela.

'On deer, sire.'

'Fia …. They attack on Fia?' Mustela bellowed.

Mustela looked out through a portal in the rock, seeing the newly raised army of Ullaunites from the vats, cut swathes through his army of Robusti and meeting up with Gannymeade's army of deer in the middle of the Robustopolis. At the head of the attack, he saw Gannymeade herself – with her returners in hand – selectively clearing her path of his Lictorial officer class, leaving the remainder in chaos, and directionless. He watched in dismay as Robusti were tossed like chaff to the wind by deer with their antlers.

To west of the mountain, Alba led a force. On one side was her sister, Olor on the other. Along the charge, Alba became unseated from her deer as it was taken down by an aggressive Robusti defence. The mob surrounded her, and she immediately fought as best she could, calling to her sister for assistance. Niamh looked up and saw her sister's plight, but knew she couldn't get to her in time before she would be over run.

The cold realisation had hardly dawned on her when she saw Olor on the move, cutting swathes through the massed ranks of Robusti. With Boudicca's Fia beneath him, clearing a path with its antlers as they went, Olor reached down and lifted up a Lictor by the scruff his neck, whom he recognized and knew as Jeybor. Olor knocked him out clinically with repeated short, but powerful punches. Taking out his returner, Olor drew the blade across his hand. Blood and Anam oil flowed from the wound. Immediately, he smeared the mixture on the Lictor's punch drunk face, who was now coming around. With that, Olor stood on the Fia's still-running back and slipped himself beneath the arm of the Lictor.

Alba was fighting furiously amongst the mob and truly thought her time had come. The numbers were overwhelming her and she knew she wouldn't survive without assistance. Just then she looked up and saw Olor and the groggy Lictor launch themselves from the Fia's back and land right beside her, in the middle of the bloody melee. Olor let the Lictor go, who now stood before the salivating hordes, dripping with Anam oil and Ullanite blood.

'Anam, Anam, Anam!' shouted Olor, as he pointed to the bewildered Lictor. They smelled the oil that covered the creature. Instinctual violence took over.

'Hold on,' said Olor, to Alba, as they jumped out of the mob, landing on the back of the Fia with acrobatic ease.

'Thank you,' said Alba, as they rode on.

Olor nodded and said nothing.

Mustela could not believe his eyes. 'We must retreat to the Dal,' he commanded. As he made his exit, he turned to Decima. 'Kill them – and join me there.'

Decima nodded and redrew her sword.

'Excuse me?' A little voice echoed around the cavern making Mustela stop in his tracks.

'Who said that?' he boomed.

'I did,' said the little voice again, clear and crisp.

Mustela cocked his head slightly as Boudicca stepped over the slumped figures of Finn and Constantina, and walked towards him, staring.

'My name is Boudicca Moriarty. You have my mother and I want her back,' she announced calmly.

'Oh, yes … the Ullaunite with the limp, I've heard of you.' The corners of his mouth turned upwards. 'You have her eyes.' Mustela quickly spun around on his plinth of weasels. With raised hands, he conjured another mound of rodents to grow beside him.

From the squealing mound, a sleeping figure emerged slowly, draped in a plain white muslin dress without any adornments – Boudicca's mother – Sarah Moriarty. The first time she had seen her in days.

'She talks of you much,' said Mustela, grinning.

'Let her go,' Boudicca demanded.

'I'm afraid you are not in a position to dictate terms,' he coolly replied. Mustela then gestured to his Praetorian enforcer. 'You must dance with my beautiful Decima. The question is, can you dance?'

The Praetorian afforded herself a rare smile as she looked at the ungainly child.

'Let my mother go.'

'Make me,' countered Mustela, raising his eyebrows. 'Make me.'

The Praetorian made the first move, coming at Boudicca with her raised scimitar. Boudicca stood motionless and calm. Decima drove her full weight into the swing in order to cleave Boudicca in two. Sparks flew as her curved blade was met with a parry from Boudicca's returner. Decima paused to review her opponent – and attacked again.

The fighting was fierce and prolonged as tempered metal met magical sheoak, the sound of clangs, thuds and thrusts filled the air. In the midst of another parry, Boudicca punched Decima across her very surprised face, drawing black blood from the side of her mouth. The Praetorian was left smarted and flummoxed, unsure of what to do next. Each attempt to cut Boudicca in two failed. Growing angry and confused, Decima began to froth at the mouth and bulge at the eye. Boudicca remained unruffled, holding her stance calm.

'Kill her!' screamed an apoplectic Mustela.

The Praetorian growled and lurched forward again. Boudicca steadied herself, and once more parried her opponent's violent and over thrown lunge. As she did, she saw Mustela and her mother begin to disappear in a haze of blue light. He was fleeing and taking her mother with him. If she didn't act now, Boudicca thought, her mother could be lost forever.

Boudicca parried, fighting Decima to a punch-drunk standstill. Looking up she saw Mustela disappearing with her mother. An eruption of emotion rose from Boudicca's gut to her chest, and then to her throat. She let out a sound that should not have come from a twelve-year-old girl but from a beast that lived in ancient times, spending millennia hiding in the darkness. Those who heard it likened it to nothing they had ever heard before. It was as pitiful as it was bestial. It frightened everyone that heard it. Even Mustela. Still, he couldn't resist taking one last look, thinking the sound to be death throe. Instead, he looked straight into her face. Where freckles had been visible on her forehead, pinholes of light now emerged, as if a constellation of stars was being emitted from her skin. Mustela eyes widened in fear.

Leaving the half-dead Decima behind, Boudicca grabbed her second returner from its sheath. Her eyes focused on one spot, the weeping letter "I" on Mustela's chest, next to his heart. Seeing her immanent attack, Mustela turned, morphed into a blue mist. Boudicca lunged into the haze with her returner. She felt the blade invade his flesh, digging into the bone of his shoulder. She thrust her weapon again, but this time she felt no resistance. As the tip of her returner vanished into the hazy blueness, so too did Mustela and Sarah.

'Don't go. Don't go!' she cried. Boudicca had never felt such hopelessness than at that moment. She knew that she had missed her target and maybe the chance to get her mother back. As the haze disappeared, she turned to see Decima also disappearing – into a dark cloud that was lost to the shadows.

By now, Constantina and Finn had regained consciousness and had been watching Decima's near annihilation in awe. They immediately ran to Boudicca's side.

'How did you do that?' asked Finn, incredulously.

Boudicca wasn't listening.

'My mother is gone,' said Boudicca. 'I have failed.'

'Failed. That's the last thing you've done, Boudicca Moriarty.' Constantina reassured her.

'But Mustela has taken her.'

'True but he saw the way you fought Decima, as we did. Your mother has come to be more valuable to him. She's now a much safer prisoner than before,' Finn explained.

'You have done well, young Boudicca Moriarty,' exclaimed Constantina.

They were both wrapping their arms around her in embrace when the stone at the cave entrance rolled back. In rode the rest of the Asio clan mounted on their Fia, all except Tarquin.

'Where is Tarquin?' asked Finn.

'He has returned to Old Joe, he needs his son at this time, to mourn for Isha,' said Tycho, alighting his Fia.

'What of the attack?' Finn asked.

'We have driven them beyond Colors Gorge. They are in disarray, retreating to the Dal,' declared an exuberant Niamh Sciurus.

'This was just a battle, the war lies ahead,' Gannymeade cautioned.

Everyone noted it. It was only then that Finn and Constantina noticed Olor standing at the door. Instinctively, they reached for their returners.

'No,' commanded Alba. 'He is us.'

Olor didn't wish to enter the chamber, uncomfortable at the memories it held for him, but Alba encouraged him forward and he stood beside her.

'Somnia Sine Metu, Boudicca Moriarty,' said Gannymeade, with a smile.

Boudicca replied with a nod, tinged with deep regret.

◆　　✦　　◆

Sometime later at Cumann Rock, the entire Asio clan moved off and gathered at the lake for the Sacring. This was a ritual ceremony that had been performed since the dawn of Ullaunite time. It called for an offering of seeds and saplings to the great emblem of nature itself: The Bradán – the great salmon of the lake. Giving thanks for the safe return of cherished clan members from the vats was uppermost in their thoughts, as well as replenishing the Anam in themselves.

'Let us rejuvenate the Bradán and ourselves,' intoned Gannymeade.

A fire of deadwood roared on the lakeside. A gentle wind pushing it left and right, it's orange glow skimming off the stillness of the lake Gannymeade retreated to a great mound of seed that the Ullaunites had been collecting. She took a handful from the mound and threw it on the fire. Boudicca looked on in silence and thought of her mother.

No words were spoken, just eyes reflecting the light and the dancing shadows it cast. It took some moments for the rest of the seed in the mound to glow. The light from the mound, competed with that of the fire and soon the seeds became weightless, floating up, in their ones and twos at first, like slow moving sparks that climbed higher, wafting into the air. The mound then ignited, sending flames twenty or so metres skyward, holding in a circular pattern above the lake. The sparks joined together in a fast-paced spin, gravity increasing with its mass and growing into a bright globe. The ball of spinning light hung there perfectly formed, fiery seed transforming in steady rotation.

In the radiant fusion of white light, Boudicca saw colours reveal themselves. She spied Gannymeade's face in concentration. Other faces were also lit by this pygmy moon above the lake. All waiting for the Bradán to come.

Swirls and eddies on the water – faint at first – began to grow in size. A spinning light bounced off scales that moved beneath the level, suggesting a behemoth below the surface of the lake. The Bradán. It was coming, from the depths, as it had always done.

Boudicca saw it appear, the light now ample enough to reveal the fullness of its size. The gargantuan salmon rose from the depths. It emerged with a mighty leap and swam effortlessly above the lake, treating the air like water. Circling the glowing seed and opening its jaws wide. It considered the ball of glowing seed a moment and then swallowed it whole. But the light did not die away. It grew even more radiant in the salmon's belly, and pulsed around its body to the extremity of its fins. The fish began to fracture. Each scale taking on a glow and forming itself into a cluster of small star-like lights that floated off, without any preordained path. Floating up to the numinous heavens above the lake.

All who gathered were covered in a glow and were healed of whatever pain afflicted them. The Ullaunites rescued from the vats. Old Joe of his grief. Olor. Gannymeade. Boudicca marvelled at the sight and before long the salmon was gone. All that remained were low-lying starlight above their heads.

•         ✛         •

Back at Cumann Rock, in a quiet moment Boudicca moved to Gannymeade.

'I wish to share a secret,' she whispered.

Gannymeade nodded and smiled.

Boudicca took off the locket and opened it with a click of her fingers and took out the tiny book she had protected for so long.

Gannymeade's eyes widened and welled. 'Megrez,' she whispered, softly.

Boudicca presented it with an open palm.

Calmly but firmly Gannymeade refused the locket. 'It is my consideration – and however hard it may seem – you have been chosen for this task.' Gannymeade bowed, her eyes clearer now. 'The book is safer with you. Collect the other books, protect them as best you can and we will protect you as best we can. And maybe … just maybe, we have a chance,' she said, with a smile. Placing her left hand over her left side of her chest. 'Juniper tea?' Gannymeade whispered.

Boudicca smiled and nodded.

# Chapter 24

The Book of Megrez

*Chapter 762*
*Verse 100*

*A cat considers*

*"It is nobler to steal than to beg; unless by begging you steal."*

In the moments after opening her eyes, Boudicca wondered if everything had been just a dream. But the sharp pain from the bump on her forehead jogged a vivid memory of falling into the river in the Chamber of Lloyb.

Boudicca woke in her grandparent's house, blankets to her chin, her head softly planted on her pillow. The bedroom, its light, and the cut flowers in the corner were all reassuringly familiar, and somehow brighter than they had ever been. She felt the locket around her neck and pulled it from beneath her pyjamas. Opening it, the book was still there. Boudicca smiled to herself.

She limped down the hall, through the kitchen, and out into the warm summer sunlight. She got a wave from Nonie who was busy in her vegetable garden, flanked by Maurice Fitzgerald who lounged nearby, lying on his side in the grass. In the yard, Boudicca could see Prospero and Paddy Kennedy leading around the chestnut mare. It was no longer suffering the shakes. The horse looked sprightly, the fever broken. Paddy was manfully trying to put money in Prospero's hand. But Prospero kept pulling his hand away, claiming to have been overpaid the last time. Paddy replying that Prospero had said the exact same thing the last time he'd visited with a sick animal. Soft threats were traded and banked by the old friends.

A quick tap on his car roof beckoned Paddy on his way. 'He's a marvel, your grandfather – an absolute marvel!' shouted Paddy, to Boudicca, from the open car window.

Boudicca waved his battered yellow Cortina and blue horse-box out of the yard, and sauntered back to the house with her grandparents. 'Still working your magic, I see,' said Boudicca.

Maurice Fitzgerald now sat in his seat beside the fireplace. Nonie and Prospero sat at the kitchen table, looking at Boudicca without saying a word.

'What?'

Her grandparents shared a glance.

'What?' repeated Boudicca, sensing their angst.

'There was a letter this morning,' said Prospero, 'addressed to you. In your mother's handwriting.

Boudicca's eyes widened, and her back straightened.

Prospero nodded to Nonie, who took it out of the pocket of her apron. Boudicca took it and held it reverentially in both hands. She saw the writing on the letter, and knew it immediately to be her mother's hand. She looked at the date stamp. It was sent the day before she went missing. Boudicca looked to her grand-parents. They were nervous about urging her on with their eyes, so they cast glances elsewhere. Boudicca opened it, slipping her finger into the gap of the envelope and tearing at it mercilessly. There was a page inside. She took it out slowly. All were bound in silence. Opening the folded page and to her confusion, she found a small card and on was written.

'Lightenings Armada.'

'Lightenings Armada?' exclaimed Prospero, in disbelief.

Boudicca looked at it again carefully, wondering if she had missed something, checking the empty envelope for more. She handed it over to Nonie, who scanned it.

'I'm baffled,' said Nonie.

'We'll have to ponder this one. I'll make tea,' offered Prospero.

Boudicca considered the card and wondered why it was sent? It was obviously a message from her mother to her, and she knew she would be with her grandparents in Kerry.

Just then the half door of the cottage, creaked open.

Prospero turned his head. 'Hello?' he called, thinking someone outside not wishing to disturb.

To their collective amazement, Finn, the wild hare had returned. Slowly he hopped in the door.

'Well, by jingos. Wild is as wild does,' said Nonie, with a smile.

He waited at the door and looked behind him. A moment later, a leveret followed him, standing close to Finn.

'He have company,' said Prospero, filling the kettle. 'A baby hare. Female too.'

Boudicca was delighted to see Finn. He hopped towards Boudicca's chair with the leveret in close attendance.

'Isn't she gorgeous?' exclaimed Nonie.

'What will we call her lads?' Announced Prospero, as if putting it to a vote.

'I know her name,' said Boudicca, as she bent down, the leveret hopping into her hands. Boudicca held her close to her chest, the baby hare comfortable and relaxed there.

'Ashket,' said Boudicca.

'Ashket?' said Prospero, with a raised lip. 'Strange name, that!'

'It suits her,' said Nonie.

Finn hopped to the chair on which Maurice Fitzgerald lay. The hare rose onto his back legs and squeaked. Maurice ignored him. Finn climbed the cushion and thumped his foot twice. Maurice Fitzgerald thought better of it and moved indignantly to the other chair with a lazy, slow stride. The sound of water boiled behind them, the kettle switch clicked, and the boiling eased.

After drinking her tea, Boudicca rose from the table, the eyes of her grandparents and Maurice Fitzgerald on her. She limped slowly down the hallway with the leveret in her hands. Finn alighted from the chair and hopped after her. Boudicca waited for him to enter her bedroom and then closed the door to the world.

The end.

Seventeen year old Jake Rollins' life is a nightmare. His dad is determined to use his family as a punching bag and Jake is powerless to stop him.

Urban gritty meets magical realism in this coming-of-age story about what it means to be bigger than where you come from.

*Can the Real JR Stand Up, Please* is a gripping and at times confronting read; a roller-coaster ride, yet a hopeful novel about being true to yourself and learning to be brave.

Perfect for readers who love a dose of magic with their realism.

The novel is lovely, …and there is something of the rebel — if not in JR, yet — in the narrator or the way the story exposes some things not often treated as a theme or central idea.

*Michele Drouart, Editor and Author*

*"This is the way the world is fed."*

The year is 2066 and life in Greenland is much warmer, more crowded, and lacking in fresh food when sixteen-year-old Jonnie lives in the relocation city of Shamed. Hundred-story towers house extended families from American coastal cities relocated after the Sixth Sea Rise. Work and school are conducted from overcrowded apartments and homeless people camp out in the streets. Jonnie's parents run a high-tech call center where family members work day and night. She shares a bedroom with her much older nieces. For quiet and privacy, Jonnie retreats to the empty rooftop. She identifies as a girl but is intersex.

Red is a homeless man who takes up temporary residence in a pigeon coop on the roof. After Red talks about seeds in the birds' droppings, Jonnie gets interested in heirloom seeds. She knows little about how food grows because meals come in packages ordered online and delivered by drone. Dishes are manufactured in the home using 3D printers.

Armed with a new understanding of old-fashioned garden-grown food, Jonnie is determined to create her own garden on the roof of her building. Along the way, she meets a former cryosphere scientist, a botanist with an urban indoor garden, and Drew and Darr, twins her own age who live in the next building. Darr is also intersex and identifies as a boy.

Jonnie's search for who she is and what she might be able to offer the world is one that will resonate with readers of all ages. The information she learns about healthy food, sustainable agriculture, and urban gardens may inspire readers to start their own gardens.

A cautionary tale with depth and humor, A Garden on Top of the World is environmental fiction for ages 12 and up. Includes resources on gardening, urban gardens, heirloom seeds, and organic foods.

**Jenna's Truth**

NADIA L. KING

aixi books

Our closest friends are the people we trust the most. We tell them our secrets and share our lives with them. But, what happens if our friends and our secrets turn against us? Jenna's Truth, inspired by Amanda Todd's tragic story of bullying, is a book that tells us what can happen when we discover our friends are no longer who we think they are.

The internet age offers many opportunities and makes life easier, but it also put us in great danger. Every post creates a digital trail that can't always be erased.

Nadia L. King has woven together a contemporary teenage story, a lesson of empathy and self-awareness, and a tale about the dangers of digital life to create a book that is utterly captivating. Jenna's Truth is both bleak and full of hope.

...amazing, honest, pure, true. I am and always will be saddened by Amanda's story, but Jenna's Truth gives us an alternate version filled with hope.

*KEVIN HINES* - Suicide survivor, activist, storyteller, filmmaker

I meant to email last week to say that at last your wonderful book was next in line on my books to read pile. And I read it in one sitting! I was so impressed by how you tackled such a challenging subject. Congratulations Nadia, it's a powerful little novella.

*DIANNE WOLFER* - Australian award-winning children's author

Inspired by the real-life story of the late Canadian teenager Amanda Todd, this story puts a human face on cyberbullying...A deeply affecting, valuable story and educational tool.

*KIRKUS REVIEW*